EYE OF THE PHARAOH

NANCY FRASER

SOUL MATE PUBLISHING

New York

EYE OF THE PHARAOH

Copyright©2016

NANCY FRASER

Cover Design by Wren Taylor

This book is a work of fiction. The names, characters, places, and incidents are the products of the author's imagination or are used fictitiously. Any resemblance to actual events, business establishments, locales, or persons, living or dead, is entirely coincidental.

All rights reserved. No part of this publication may be reproduced, stored in a retrieval system, or transmitted in any form or by any means (electronic, mechanical, photocopying, recording, or otherwise) without the prior written permission of both the copyright owner and the publisher. The only exception is brief quotations in printed reviews.

The scanning, uploading, and distribution of this book via the Internet or via any other means without the permission of the publisher is illegal and punishable by law. Please purchase only authorized electronic editions, and do not participate in or encourage electronic piracy of copyrighted materials.

Your support of the author's rights is appreciated.

Published in the United States of America by
Soul Mate Publishing
P.O. Box 24
Macedon, New York, 14502

ISBN: 978-1-68291-210-2

ebook ISBN: 978-1-68291-222-5

www.SoulMatePublishing.com

The publisher does not have any control over and does not assume any responsibility for author or third-party websites or their content.

A Note From the Author ...

As an author and a woman I am attracted to all sorts of romantic heroes. Sure, they should be drop-dead gorgeous and sexy as sin but, more importantly, they should be compassionate, witty, and intelligent. And possess an imperfection or two.

That was my goal in creating Dr. Joshua Cain, Professor of Archaeology and Art History. In *Eye of the Pharaoh,* Dr. Cain spouts ancient history with the ease of a confident educator. With the exception of the fictitious Anukehaten, guardian of the Queen-Pharaoh Hatshepsut's tomb, and the ancient curse of the pink stone and statue, all historical references shared by Dr. Cain are accurate depictions of Egyptian culture and hierarchy.

My goal for my heroine, Teri Hunter, was to create an attractive, equally intelligent professional with some quirky habits. Teri is a walking motivational quote, often dredging up one of those commonplace office posters when she needs a bit of emotional reinforcement. She's even taken her personal mantra from one of her favorites: Wake Up. Kick Ass. Repeat.

She's often heard quoting the likes of First Lady Eleanor Roosevelt, author/clothing designer Donna Karan, comedian Louis C.K., and even Albert Einstein.

My personal favorite comes from author Mason Cooley: Romance is tempestuous. Love is calm. It's a mantra I strive for when creating every happily-ever-after.

I hope you enjoy reading *Eye of the Pharaoh* as much as I enjoyed writing it. If you're looking for a huge 'black moment' you may be disappointed. However, I'm a believer that finding true love takes many paths and not all of them are filled with angst. Some are filled with curses and mummies and hot Egyptian nights!

I love hearing from readers. You can find me on Facebook under NancyFraserAuthor, or on Twitter @nfraserauthor. And, if you're so inclined, I also love receiving honest reviews.

Nancy

This book is dedicated to the memory of my good friend Patti Shenberger who, prior to her passing, was my sounding board for all things ancient and spooky. You would have loved seeing this one published, Patti, because it would mean I'd finally stop bugging you about scarabs and sarcophagi!

Acknowledgements

A huge thank you to Debby Gilbert for editing and publishing a book that has taken me forever to complete.

Another big thanks to artist Wren Taylor for my beautiful cover. And, to all the other Soul Mate professionals who were part of producing this novel.

Finally, a whole lot of love for my sons, daughters-in-law and grandchildren who put up with my flights of fancy and requests to 'go away and leave me alone' so I can write.

Chapter 1

Department of Art and Archaeology
Princeton University

Wake up. Kick ass. Repeat.
Teri Hunter mouthed the motivational phrase she'd chosen for her personal mantra as she stepped across the threshold into the dark and musty storeroom.

A dim light shone from a glass-enclosed workroom in the far corner. Taking a tentative step forward, she faltered when the floorboards creaked beneath her feet. Something fast and furry brushed against her ankle. A shiver ran down her back, yet she fought the urge to retreat.

Do one thing every day that scares you.

This was obviously today's obstacle. Were it not for her professional commitments and intricately organized schedule, she'd have no doubt bolted for the door and returned to the safety and illumination of the main building.

'Sorry, but the storage area doesn't have overhead lighting. Preservation of the antiquities. You understand.' The dean's words echoed in her head. What little outside light there was had become nearly non-existent due to an impending thunderstorm.

Drawing a deep breath, she took a second step and then a third, winding her way past a half-dozen crates, some open, some not. To her left she heard a rustling of paper; to her right the distinct sound of footsteps.

Her apprehension grew, the hair on her forearms stood

at attention. She'd barely made it halfway across the room before bumping into something large and solid. Reaching out, she laid her hand against the oversized object. Slowly, she raised her head and came face to face with the painted mask of an Egyptian noble. The chipped finish gave the death mask a deranged look.

"You come here often, big boy?" A nervous giggle followed her softly-worded, albeit silly, question and she pressed her fingertips to her lips to stifle an outright laugh before lowering her hand to her side.

Go big! Home is boring.

Silently she cursed her habit of dredging up poster-worthy quotes to mask her fears.

Sidestepping her way around the ancient sarcophagus, Teri moved closer to the light. That was when she saw him.

Dr. Joshua Cain.

Bent over his workbench, he held an ornate canopic jar in one hand. Using what appeared to be a horsehair brush, he worked diligently at cleaning away thousands of years of accumulated dirt.

She couldn't see his face, yet his shoulders were broad. His hair, dark brown with a hint of gray, brushed the collar of his lab coat.

He shifted on the stool, inching closer to the overhead lamp. When he turned the jar over in his hands, Teri was mesmerized by the gentle way his long fingers caressed the priceless object. Beneath the sleeves of her silk blouse, her skin tingled. She waited for him to place the jar on the workbench before clearing her throat, coughing softly to get his attention.

He turned on the stool, his head bent, his attention on . . . of all things . . . her feet. Inside her sensible, three-inch heels, her toes curled.

He raised his head slowly, his gaze running over her like

water from a warm rain shower. Their gazes met briefly, his brown eyes magnified by the protective goggles he wore. His jaw, covered with the stubble of a day-old beard, was square, his lips full and turned down in an obvious frown of disapproval. Intent on studying his face, she was immediately drawn to the scar running from ear to chin.

How had he gotten it? Which of his many adventures had given him yet another layer to his rugged good looks?

"How in the devil do you expect to work in that outfit?" he asked, his voice deeper, richer than she'd expected.

Teri glanced down at her suit, the pencil-straight skirt hugging her knees. "Excuse me?"

"I said—"

"I heard what you said, Dr. Cain," she clarified. "I just don't understand why my choice of clothing should matter?"

"How do you expect to empty dust-covered crates dressed like an uptight librarian?"

"Empty crates?" she repeated.

"Yes, that's what you were sent here to do, wasn't it?"

"Uh, no." Taking a step closer to where he sat, she held out her hand. "I'm Teri Hunter."

He didn't shake her offered hand, but rather turned back to his workbench. "If you're not the graduate student I sent for, then what are you doing here? This is a highly restricted area."

"Like I said, I'm Teri Hunter, and—"

"If your name is supposed to mean something to me, Miss Hunter, it doesn't. Now, if you're not here to work, I'd appreciate it if you'd leave. I've got no time for small talk. I'm on a very tight schedule."

"I know," said told him. "That's why I'm here. I'm your publicist."

He turned back to face her, his previous frown deepening to a full-on scowl. "My publicist? What the devil would I want with a publicist?"

She squared her shoulders and met his darkened glare. "I don't believe it has anything to do with what you want, Dr. Cain. It's what your publisher wants."

"Well, you can go back to the publisher and tell them I don't need a publicist. I've been doing lectures for years. I know the drill."

"Lectures yes, but not book tours. This, for all intents and purposes, is a book tour with a bit of lecturing thrown in for good measure."

"I'm confident I can handle both."

Teri drew a deep breath, searching for the best way to explain the value of having someone there to guide him through the intricacies of a multi-city tour. "As I'm sure you're aware Dr. Cain, *The Pharaoh's Mummy* is quickly climbing nearly every non-fiction bestseller list in the country. With my help, you can easily become number one on every list that counts."

Rather than show his enthusiasm at the mention of topping the bestseller lists, his scowl grew wider. His expression reminded her of the façade on the timeworn sarcophagus, imperfect yet commanding.

"And just what *exactly* does a publicist do, Miss Hunter?"

"I'll be accompanying you on the tour, and making sure everything runs smoothly. I'll meet with the bookstores to ensure the signings are well publicized, with the museum staff to coordinate the lectures times, and, of course, I'll arrange for a few television interviews and cocktail receptions along the way. Other than that, you'll never know I'm there."

Teri could have sworn she heard him mumble a very ungentlemanly expletive.

Joshua Cain held up the canopic jar he'd been cleaning earlier and asked, "Do you have any idea what this is, Miss Hunter?"

She took a step closer to where he sat, stretched out her hand, her fingertips hovering over yet not touching the gold-encrusted top. "It's a canopic jar, made of limestone, possibly from the late eighteenth dynasty. The head on this jar represents Hapi, the baboon."

He nodded once in acknowledgement. "You know your Egyptian history, Miss Hunter. I'm somewhat impressed."

"I make it my business to know everything necessary when I'm about to represent a client."

He stared at her, his eyebrows arched in surprise or, possibly, disbelief. "Everything?" he asked, a half-smile rearranging his features, softening an otherwise stoic expression.

"For instance, I know you're a tenured professor at the University with PhDs in both archaeology and art history. You're thirty-six, a widower with two daughters, ages eight and eleven. Every summer you travel to either South America or Egypt on a dig in search of priceless treasures."

"Anything else?"

"You're considered one of the world's foremost experts in the identification, authentication, and preservation of Egyptian artifacts." She paused for a moment, then added, "And, rumor has it, you're deathly afraid of spiders."

He laughed, the simple gesture lifting the corners of his mouth into an even broader smile.

"That I am, Miss Hunter. That I am." Turning his back to her, he said, "If you don't mind, I've got to get to work. These pieces aren't going to clean themselves."

"As much as I'd like to stay and watch, I'll get out of your way. I've got a dozen things to do before Wednesday."

"Wednesday?"

It was her turn to laugh and she did so easily. "Wednesday, Dr. Cain. The airplane, the book tour, the Big Easy."

"Oh, yeah, right. That."

Shaking her head, she left him to his work. Turning this obviously brilliant, yet seemingly absent minded, professor into a best-selling author was likely going to be the challenge of her rising career.

You didn't wake up today to be mediocre.

A brief, self-indulgent smile lifted the corners of her mouth. If there was one thing she loved, it was a challenge.

Chapter 2

Museum of Art
New Orleans, Louisiana

"Dr. Cain, it is truly a pleasure to meet you." The museum curator offered her hand in greeting and he clasped it gently.

"As I am to meet you, Mrs. DeChambeau. I am a huge fan of your late husband's work in art history. He will be greatly missed."

Teri stood off to the side, surprised yet impressed with this softer side of Joshua Cain. He'd been all business on the morning flight. So much so, he'd booked the first class seat beside his own for his books, briefcase, and the mysterious, locked box he'd carried on board. She'd been relegated to the seat across the aisle and subjected to the ramblings of a man claiming to be the reincarnation of a voodoo priest. By the time they'd landed in New Orleans, she'd had a headache the size of Jackson Square.

"I understand you're staying at Collingwood," Mrs. DeChambeau said. "It's such a beautiful and historic home."

"I try to stay there whenever I'm in New Orleans," he told her. "The city just isn't the same unless you stay in the French Quarter."

Teri turned her attention to the museum's display, numerous pieces of Egyptian history gathered for the occasion. Although they weren't currently featuring the items on a regular basis, the museum had made an admirable effort at pulling some impressive pieces from their archives.

One display area just behind the speaker's podium sat empty and Teri wondered if that was where Dr. Cain would put the items from his locked box.

Chairs were set up in the open area and another table sat to the right of the podium, the pristine white tablecloth covered with copies of Dr. Cain's book, *The Pharaoh's Mummy*.

"Dr. Cain," Mrs. DeChambeau began, "I'm sure you want to get checked into your rooms so you can freshen up before the evening's festivities. I'll have our driver take you there whenever you're ready."

"That would be wonderful, thank you. In the meantime, I'd like to put something in the museum's safe." He lifted the box up and rested it on the edge of the closest table.

"Surely, if you'll come with me."

Joshua Cain followed the woman down a narrow corridor to the left, Teri a few steps behind. When they reached the vault area, Mrs. DeChambeau raised her hand to the identification pad to gain admittance.

"State-of-the-art security," he commented. "I like that."

He placed the case inside a safe deposit box within the huge vault and waited for the curator to close and lock the door. She handed him the key and he stuck it in the pocket of his jeans.

"Dr. Cain, I have a favor to ask."

He turned to face the older woman. "Yes, what is it?"

"While we were cataloging the archives and choosing pieces for our display, I came across an item not listed anywhere on our inventory."

"What type of item?"

"A stone, clear pink, but not like any jewel I'm familiar with." Lowering her voice to a whisper, she added, "I believe it belonged to my husband because it was in a plain brown box with his handwriting on the top."

"What did it say?" he asked.

"That's part of the puzzle, I'm afraid. The writing is faded and barely discernible. I was only able to make out a few words and they made no sense whatsoever."

"May I see the stone?"

"It's not here. I took it home." Mrs. DeChambeau met his serious gaze. "I know I shouldn't have, but it doesn't appear to belong to the museum. I wanted an assessment of its origin and of how it came to be here before I decide what to do with it."

"Will you bring the item this evening?"

"Yes. Perhaps you can examine it after your lecture and book signing."

A short nod preceded his agreement. "It would be my pleasure."

Teri stared in amazement at the well-worn guest home Dr. Cain had chosen for their stay. In her mind's eye, she could see the grand entranceway of the Marriott on Canal Street, feel the pampered luxury of the hotel spa. Instead, she got this... an early nineteenth-century home in obvious need of repair. Collingwood, apparently, had history. Of what, she wasn't certain. From the road, it looked like something torn from the pages of a horror novel.

"This is where we're staying?" she asked, unable to hide her disappointment.

"You're welcome to go elsewhere, if you'd like. Personally, I prefer a room with some character."

She choked back an outright laugh. "It's certainly got character. As a matter of fact, *Freddie Kruger* comes to mind."

He shot her a disapproving frown before taking his bags from the driver and starting up the front walkway. Teri had no choice but to follow. They'd barely made it to the porch when the huge oak door opened. A short, frail-looking woman stood in the entryway.

"Welcome back, Joshua," the woman greeted.

"Thank you, Martha. It's good to be here." Glancing back to where Teri stood, he said, "This is Miss Hunter. She's with me."

"Oh," the woman said simply. "Welcome, Miss Hunter. We trust your stay here at Collingwood will be enjoyable."

Teri smiled faintly, but couldn't muster up a 'thank you' to save her soul.

"One room or two, Joshua?"

In unison, they both answered, "Two."

Martha responded with a minute bob of her graying head and then motioned toward the parlor with a sweep of her hand. "We were just about to have tea if you'd care to join us."

"If you don't mind," Dr. Cain began, "we'd like to get situated in our rooms. We've got an event at the museum tonight and I, for one, would like a bit of down time to work on my lecture."

"You're in your usual room. I can give Miss Hunter the room next to yours, if you'd like."

He shook his head. "Perhaps she would be more comfortable across the hall with a view of the garden."

"As you wish, Joshua."

Teri followed closely behind as they climbed the stairs to the second floor. She was about to turn toward the long hallway when she realized they were climbing yet another flight. What she wouldn't give for an elevator or even a bellman. Rather than voice her wishes, she hiked her carry-on higher up on her shoulder and tugged on the handle of her suitcase until the wheels gained purchase on the worn carpet. The next landing looked to be at least a half-mile away.

When they reached the third floor, Martha stopped outside the first room off the staircase and opened the door. "This is your room, Miss Hunter."

Dr. Cain had already crossed the hallway and opened

the door to the room just opposite hers. Teri took a short step forward. "Thank you."

"Bathroom is down the hall," Martha told her, the woman's simple statement stopping Teri dead in her tracks.

"Down the hall?" she asked. "You mean there's no bathroom in my suite?"

Martha chuckled heartily, her wrinkled cheeks jiggling and sagging like warm Jell-O. "Child, there's no suite in your suite, it's just a room. And, everyone shares the facilities." Nodding toward the end of the long hallway, she added, "The key hangs outside the door. You take it in with you, lock the door from the inside, and try not to take longer than fifteen minutes."

Teri gave her hostess a half-hearted smile. Closing the door behind her, she pulled her suitcase to the far side of the room. Against one wall there was a huge, four-poster bed. An ornately carved dresser sat against the opposite wall complete with a Victorian bowl and pitcher. Teri leaned forward until she could look beneath the bed, fully expecting to find a chamber pot hidden by the ruffles of the handmade quilt. All she found were dust bunnies.

Double-shuttered windows overlooked a beautiful garden, totally at odds with the chipped paint and rusted ironwork of the old home. Teri unlatched the window and pushed it open. The heavy scent of magnolias wafted in on a slight breeze. Taking a seat in a nearby chair, she put her feet up on the cushioned footstool and laid her head back for a few moments of welcome relaxation.

She awoke with a start, surprised to find she'd actually dozed off. The sound of someone moving down the corridor outside her room had her immediately alert. Tentatively, she crossed the room and opened her door a crack to see who it was.

The sight that greeted her caused her breath to catch and, somewhat unexpectedly, her pulse to race. Joshua Cain was coming down the hall from the bathroom, clad in little more than a towel, the wiry hairs on his chest still glistening with water from his shower. It looked as if he'd finger-combed his hair into place, yet a few longer strands dangled rather rakishly across his forehead.

Teri realized she'd been caught staring when he looked up and met her gaze through the narrow opening. He didn't bother to acknowledge her but, rather, turned and went into his room, shutting the door behind him. The click of the lock echoed in the hallway.

She checked the time on her PDA and realized she had less than an hour to get showered and dressed before their rented town car would arrive to pick them up. Gathering her bathrobe, clean underwear, and toiletries, she slipped out of her room and down the hall toward the shared bath. Opening the door, she came face to face with an old claw-foot tub. No shower, no guest shampoo or fancy, individually wrapped soaps. The luxury room she'd been wishing for earlier seemed even farther away than it had before.

Josh slipped into his sport coat and adjusted his tie. They were scheduled to leave at any minute and he had yet to hear from the efficient Miss Hunter. He'd half-expected her to be tapping on his door before now, double-checking to make sure he was ready for his first lecture and book signing.

Although he'd not intended it, he couldn't help but wonder what she'd be wearing. She had a penchant, he noticed, for business suits; stuffy, professional, boring. He was curious as to whether or not she ever let her hair down or wore jeans and sweatshirts. Had she ever considered trekking through the stifling heat in search of a centuries-old relic? Somehow, he doubted it. The prim Miss Hunter seemed more like the cubicle and air-conditioning type.

A smile tugged at the corners of his mouth when he

remembered how flustered she'd been negotiating three flights of stairs in her heels, dragging her suitcase behind her. She hadn't said anything, but the firm set of her mouth spoke volumes in itself. The memory brought another thought to mind.

Just exactly how soft were those pouty, perfectly formed lips?

Josh shook his head, dislodging the wayward and totally unwanted vision. It had been a while since he'd been attracted to a woman, and even longer since he actually been with one. And, unfortunately, his current dry spell showed no signs of letting up anytime soon.

Not that he wanted it to. He had a plan. For his work, his daughters, and his immediate future. None of them included becoming involved with a woman. Even one as undeniably smart and attractive as Teri Hunter.

After New Orleans, they were scheduled to go to Chicago, Boston, Baltimore, and New York. Two weeks on the road with someone who, despite his efforts to ignore her, kept creeping into his thoughts.

The knock he'd been expecting sounded at his door. Crossing the room, he gave the ornate glass doorknob a tug. She stood there, framed in the doorway, dressed in a sexy, red, lace-trimmed cocktail dress, her long blond hair combed back at the sides and hanging in loose waves against her shoulders. His body responded in a most predictable fashion, an unfortunate side-effect of said dry spell.

"You look lovely this evening, Miss Hunter," he told her honestly.

"Thank you. And, please, call me Teri. If we're going to be stuck together for two weeks, we should probably be on a first-name basis."

"Fine with me," he said. "Feel free to call me Josh." Lifting his briefcase from the chair by the door, he told her, "We should probably head downstairs. The car will be here any minute."

Stuck. She thought of her job as being stuck with him. So this was what rejection felt like. Not that he'd never been rejected before but, for some insane reason, this time it bothered him. Far more than it should have.

Stuck. The one word reminded him, in no uncertain terms, theirs was a business arrangement and nothing more. Just exactly as he wanted it. Now, if his body would be as accepting as his mind, he might just survive the next couple of weeks intact.

"As you can see by the pieces in this next case," Josh began, "the seventeenth dynasty was partial to gold inlay. The use of hieroglyphics on the edge of this relief indicates an owner of high regard, most likely a Pharaoh's guard or priest. This smaller statue, found at the same location, indicates the person buried in this particular temple valued family and had fathered at least sixteen offspring."

Teri had to give it the professor, he was a commanding speaker. Not one attendee dared to pull out a phone, send a text, or excuse themselves for a break. All sat in rapt attention, hanging on his every word.

"Dr. Cain will take questions now," Mrs. DeChambeau announced.

The first hand to go up was that of a woman who'd arrived with a group of University students. "Dr. Cain, were all families in ancient Egypt so large? Did every man sire so many children?"

"No. Not every man was as prolific as the one I'd mentioned a moment ago. However, it was important for those who held high office and, especially, men of noble blood to advance their lineage as much as possible. Often, if a man was unable to produce offspring, he would be stripped of his title and treated as if he were of less value. The average

Egyptian family contained one husband, one to three wives, again depending on societal stature, and usually no more than six or seven children."

A young man raised his hand next. "In your book you devote one full chapter and part of another outlining the differences between legitimate and illegitimate succession, yet you don't explain exactly how the final decision as to the rightful heir was made. Can you elaborate?"

"Different dynasties had different ways of dealing with the issue of right of inheritance, both in position and in possession. Some of their methods are no different than those we employ today. As in modern times, they had councils and courts where each claimant would present their case. Most often the line of legitimacy could be decided by birth order, financial holdings, or even by marriage into a family of standing. Of course, sometimes it was decided by whichever son was left standing at the end of the battle. I like to think we've evolved."

The questions continued for another twenty minutes before Mrs. DeChambeau called a halt to the evening. "It is half-past ten, and far longer than we'd hoped to impose upon Dr. Cain's expertise. We wish to thank you all for a wonderful evening and ask that you give our guest one last round of applause."

Teri scanned the crowd from wall to wall. Her smile spread slowly. Turnout had been even better than they'd hoped. Nearly two hundred people packed the room. Professors, students, artists, and even what Teri pegged as groupies, young women whose interest seemed far more attuned to the professor than to the artifacts on display.

All one hundred copies of *The Pharaoh's Mummy* sold out in less than an hour and Josh patiently signed each and every one. His lecture on the importance of continued archaeological research drew a standing ovation and, as she'd hoped, she finally got to see what was inside the mysterious locked box. The beautiful, three-thousand-year-old, scarab had fascinated everyone in attendance, including her.

Once the last guest exited the room, Teri took a seat, slid out of her heels, and put her feet up, quite willing to relax while Josh and Mrs. DeChambeau huddled together at a nearby table.

"Here's the box," the curator said, handing Josh a shoebox-sized package.

Teri watched while he turned the entire bundle over and over before finally opening the lid. Inside, there was a square case, similar to a ring box with cloth cover and a hinged top. Josh raised the lid and removed the stone, cradling it in the palm of his hand.

"I know I've seen pictures of a gem similar to this," he said, "but, at the moment, I can't recall where." Holding the stone up to the light, he studied it from both sides and ran his fingers across the surface as if inspecting it for flaws.

A shiver ran down Teri's back as her gaze focused on Josh's gentle handling of the precious stone.

Mrs. DeChambeau stroked the stone with her index finger, as if drawing up a memory. "My husband brought a number of items back with him from an excavation in Brazil in nineteen-eighty, the last trip he made out of the country. I wonder if that could be where he obtained this piece."

"I don't think so," Josh said. "I'm familiar with nearly every mineral native to South America, and this is not like anything I've seen before."

"Can you make out any of the writing on the box?" Mrs. DeChambeau asked.

"At first glance, these three numbers appear to be either a page number, or perhaps part of a date. The symbol here," he said, pointing to a mark in the corner, "looks like a crude attempt at a hieroglyphic."

"Could it be some type of code?" Mrs. DeChambeau

asked.

"A code?"

"Harold had a group of friends, all ancient art and history buffs. They would often send each other notes in code in an attempt to keep their art finds, or intended purchases, from falling into the hands of their competitors."

Josh scanned the wrapping a second time before asking, "Have you spoken to any of your husband's friends about the box, or the stone?"

"Unfortunately, the last of the group passed away just a month after my husband, long before I found the box."

"Would you mind if I took everything back to Collingwood with me? I'd like to pull up some research documents I have in my department archives. For security purposes, I can only get to them through my laptop and with a pass code which I have to obtain just before logging in." When she hesitated, Josh added, "I'd be happy to either give you a receipt for the piece. Or, I could leave the scarab as collateral."

"Collateral isn't necessary. I'm sure my husband would have trusted you implicitly, as do I," she told him. "However, you are welcome to leave the scarab in the museum safe until your stay in New Orleans is complete."

Chapter 3

Teri took a seat opposite Josh in Collingwood's sun-filled breakfast room. "Good morning. You're up early, considering how late it was when we finally got back last night. I assumed you'd probably stayed up half the night researching the pink stone." She reached for the coffee pot in the middle of the table and poured herself a cup.

"I wasn't able to get onto the university's network last night to obtain a password. They were going through upgrades."

Teri chuckled. "Ah, yes, the infamous computer upgrades. A bane to anyone who wants to get something accomplished after midnight."

"What can I get for you this morning, Miss Hunter?" Martha asked. "We have egg soufflé, croissants, fresh fruit, caramel apple muffins, and a handful of packaged cereals to choose from, as well as either cranberry, apple, or fresh-squeezed orange juice."

"I'd love some orange juice and a croissant, please."

"Would you prefer apple butter or homemade marmalade for your croissant?"

"Plain is fine, thank you."

Once Martha left to get Teri's juice and pastry, Josh opened his notebook and spread it out between them. "I did manage to find some information on the last of Dr. DeChambeau's art excursions. He and a few of his friends wrote a number of papers on the proper excavation of South American artifacts. As well as at least two photo displays of the items they found and returned to the museum in Brazil."

"Was there anything in there about the gem?"

"No. Most of the items found during their trip were limestone or pottery. However, I did notice a number of the pieces released by the local government and brought back from the trip were boxed similar to the way he'd stored the stone. That may be something."

They finished their breakfast just moments before the arrival of their car.

Teri picked up her briefcase from beside the table and started toward the door. "So, Dr. Cain, are you ready for another day of smile and sign?"

He shook his head and followed closely behind. "Not really. Now that I've got a mystery of sorts to unravel, I'm much rather be at my computer working."

The first scheduled event of the morning was a book signing at one of the enclosed malls just outside New Orleans. Josh patiently answered questions, signed books, and chatted with everyone, no matter whether they were true lovers of Egyptian history, or only curious as to what could possibly have drawn such a huge crowd.

Teri stood off to the side, mentally calculating the number of books sold and signed, the reaction of the audience, and the ease with which Josh weathered the crowd. He'd been in his element the night before, lecturing, answering questions and even signing his book. Yet, for someone who had never done a public book signing before, he seemed perfectly at ease with the attention.

At half-past eleven, she threaded her way through the milling customers and put up a sign proclaiming the impending end to the event.

"Thank you," Josh whispered when she stood the placard up at the end of the table. "My hand is getting cramped."

She smiled down at him and responded, "You shouldn't have written such an interesting book, Dr. Cain."

Josh flexed his hand, the simple motion drawing her gaze like a magnet to a piece of metal, then accepted the next book. Raising his gaze to the elderly woman in line, he asked, "Who should I make this out to?"

As inconspicuously as she could, Teri slipped back into her corner. Twenty-five more minutes, a quick bite of lunch, and then they'd be on their way to the television station for Josh's first live media event.

Josh unclipped the microphone from his collar and handed it to the grip before stepping down from the stage and heading in her direction. The old adage, *If looks could kill,* came to mind when Teri met his thunderous expression.

"Who the hell preps these people?" he asked, not waiting for her comment on his way to the closest exit.

"We gave her a list of questions," she assured him, practically running to keep up with his hurried pace. "I had no idea she would stray so far off topic."

He stopped short and she nearly ran into him from behind. Turning to face her, he started to speak and then paused, as if reining in his words. Finally, he said, "I will not do another of these interviews unless I have the station manager's word that the questions will not ramble off in a direction totally at odds with the book, or archaeology. Is that clear?"

"Perfectly, and I couldn't agree more. Her personal questions were completely out of line."

"Why the devil should she care whether I'm dating someone or not? It's none of her damned business."

Rather than respond, Teri took her seat in the town car and waited for Josh to join her. A minute or two passed before she leaned out the window and asked, "Are you coming?"

He shook his head. "No, I'm not. I need to walk off some

of this anger before I go back to my research. I'll meet you at Collingwood in an hour."

"Don't forget, you're scheduled for one more book signing at four," she reminded him.

His deep sigh told her exactly what he thought of another book signing. Yet, when he could have complained, he simply said, "I'll be ready to go at three-thirty."

Teri pushed the button to close the window, shutting out Josh and his somewhat tempered anger. After telling the driver where she needed to go, she slid back into the comfort of the luxurious leather seat and replayed the past hour in her head.

Not that she blamed Josh for being upset. The female reporter had been tenacious with her line of personal questions yet glossed over both the book and Josh's reputation in the field of archaeology. Teri half-expected the woman to make an overt pass at him. Or, at the very least, slip him her phone number.

Obviously, the young groupies at the museum the night before and the more mature reporter today found Dr. Joshua Cain extremely attractive. And, if she were to be totally honest with herself, he definitely possessed a rugged *Indiana Jones* vibe about him. Even the scar added a hint of mystery while not detracting from his looks in the least. Were he not her client, she might have been attracted to him as well.

However, business was business, pleasure was pleasure. And, as she'd found out early in her career, the two definitely don't mix.

Even the briefest reminder of her near-career-ending folly made her anger rise and her heart race. She'd been young, foolish, and eager to please. The assignment . . . an up-and-coming actor on his first promotional tour. He'd been all too willing to indulge in a bit of fun and she'd been star-struck.

Dr. Cain is different.

With a sigh, Teri acknowledged her subconscious attempt at rationalization. He was different. Mature, established. Intelligent, confident. And, unfortunately, far more difficult to ignore than she'd anticipated.

Put on your big-girl panties and just do it. Another of her favorite meme quotes. She just couldn't decide whether the 'do it' meant stop or go.

Josh disconnected his cell and punched the one-time-use password into his laptop. Within seconds, data streamed onto his screen compliments of the university's extensive archives. With less than an hour and a half before he needed to change for the next book event, he intended to use his time wisely.

Not for the first time in the last few days, Josh wished he hadn't written *The Pharaoh's Mummy*, yet the ridiculous tongue-in-cheek look at both the legitimate and illegitimate heirs to Egypt's thrones had somehow captured an audience. And, if Teri Hunter's statistics were reliable, it was a huge audience. The upside to this ridiculous circus, if there was one, would obviously have to be the opportunity to reach people who'd never given archaeology or ancient Egypt a second thought. As an educator, he appreciated the idea of attracting a fresh mind to an old subject. For that reason alone, he'd forced himself to put up with his publisher's demands.

The data stream fully loaded, Josh began with the eighteenth dynasty, part of the New Kingdom period. He couldn't be certain, but the pink stone reminded him somewhat of the jewels bestowed upon Nefertiti by Akhenaten sometime between 1353 and 1334 BC. He'd search the photo archives first then move on to the inventories made by members of the expedition that discovered Nefertiti's tomb. His answer would hopefully be hidden somewhere within their records.

A little more than an hour later, Josh reluctantly set aside his research, locking his laptop with a complicated pass code and then sliding it into his briefcase along with the copious notes he'd compiled longhand. As old-fashioned as it seemed, he had to admit, he loved being able to put the loose pages together like a jigsaw puzzle in hopes of forming a random thought . . . a possible solution to his quest.

Not waiting for Teri to call for him, he slipped on his sport coat and stepped out into the hallway, nearly knocking over the efficient publicist in the process.

"Sorry," he mumbled, automatically reaching out to steady them both.

"That's okay. I wasn't watching where I was going."

Josh released the grasp he'd taken on her arms and stepped back, even the slightest contact with her soft skin causing a tingle in his hands. It was then that he noticed she'd changed her clothes from her usual business suit to a pair of casual slacks and short-sleeve blouse. Although he wasn't sure why it should matter, he found this laid-back version of Teri Hunter even more attractive than her business alter-ego or the dressed-to-the-nines persona from the evening before.

The woman was turning out to be an enticing contradiction. And a distraction, albeit an enjoyable one.

Just keep reminding yourself of your well-designed plan.

Shoving his pesky inner voice aside, he took the stairs two at a time, a smile tugging on the corners of his mouth. Plans, after all, could be revised.

Teri climbed into the waiting car and motioned for Josh to follow. "All set?"

"As ready as I'm ever going to be." He graced her with a half-smile. "I'm sorry about earlier. I shouldn't have lost my temper."

She shook her head and returned his smile. "I understand. I really do."

"I hate these things . . . the publicity and all. I'd be perfectly happy doing lectures and signings like last night, even an over-the-top signing like earlier this morning, but the whole television thing is unnerving."

Teri found his admission surprising. She'd assumed there was nothing that could rattle someone as educated, and as professionally commanding, as Josh. "Not everyone's comfortable in front of a camera," she said, hoping to erase his unease.

"It's not the cameras. I've done hundreds of interviews before. It's the self-promotion for something I'd not expected to be read by anyone other than my students and colleagues. I have to admit, I'm a bit overwhelmed by the response."

"It's a great book. It deserves an attentive audience."

He turned in the seat, his gaze meeting hers, his expression one of simple surprise. "You've read it?"

"Twice actually, cover-to-cover. The first time was simply research for my job, the second for the sheer entertainment. I had no idea there was so much promiscuity going on beneath the pyramids."

He chuckled and Teri was immediately struck by the richness of his laughter, the deep resonance in his tone.

"I left out some of the juicier parts," he told her. "I didn't want to risk it being too explicit for publication."

A warm blush rose in her cheeks. The book had been racy enough. She couldn't imagine it being even more so.

Thankfully, she was saved from commenting when they arrived at their destination. Just a few blocks off the university campus, the quaint, privately owned bookstore obviously catered to an upscale, well-educated clientele. Hopefully, the atmosphere would be more relaxed than the mega-store from earlier in the day. The huge crowd at the morning signing, followed by the interview debacle, had not been a great start to their last full day in New Orleans. If they could get through this signing and one other first thing tomorrow, they could catch their afternoon flight to Chicago and get on with the next leg in the tour.

The planned two-hour signing turned into three and a half, complete with an impromptu lecture on the history of the fourth and fifth dynasties of ancient Egypt. Teri had taken a seat in the back of the room with the intention of getting some work done. Yet she'd barely made it through a single confirming text message before being drawn into Josh's account of his last expedition and the discovery of some of the oldest remains ever found in the region.

His passion for the period, the country, and the overall history flowed smoothly with every word he spoke. If she closed her eyes, Teri could visualize the pyramids and hear the shouts of the workers as they toiled to build yet another monument to the reigning Pharaoh.

At half-past seven, Josh stood, called a halt to the lively discussion, and offered his hand to the bookstore's owner in gratitude for an enjoyable afternoon.

"It was my pleasure," the man replied. "And I know everyone here was mesmerized by your adventures."

The dozen or so people seated on chairs, the floor and the front checkout counter obviously agreed when they all stood and gave Josh an ovation. Rather sheepishly, it seemed, he nodded his thanks.

"Miss Hunter." Josh reached out and drew her to her feet. "If you're ready to go, I'm sure Mr. Abbott would like to close up for the evening."

When they'd taken their seats in the waiting town car, Teri told him, "You realize we've missed our dinner reservations."

"Not to worry. I've got an even better place in mind."

"Better than Banana's Foster for dessert?" she asked.

"How about we have dinner where I choose? Then, if you're still hungry, we can sneak into Brennan's for late dessert."

"That sounds reasonable to me," she said. Hopefully, Josh didn't choose restaurants the same way he chose his hotels.

Apparently he did.

They pulled up to a shabby-looking diner in the middle of the French Quarter and stepped out onto the curb. Josh leaned into the car and told the driver, "You can go for the evening. We'll walk back to Collingwood from here. I'm sorry we kept you so long at the bookstore." After handing the driver a sizeable tip for his inconvenience, Josh took Teri's arm and ushered her inside.

She felt as if she'd stepped back into the nineteen-fifties. The Formica countertops were worn, as if they'd been scrubbed thousands upon thousands of times. The chairs matched the pattern of the counter and tables in both design and wear. They took a seat in the first open booth, the individual jukebox catching her eye.

"I haven't seen one of these in years," she said.

"The owners probably haven't changed a thing in this place, including the music, since the day they opened."

"So, are you still hungry for Bananas Foster?" Josh asked an hour later.

She shook her head, too full to even speak.

Josh chuckled and then motioned for the check. "Two helpings of Alligator Voodoo and half a shrimp po'boy," he noted. "I haven't got a clue where you put all that food."

"Delicious," she managed to say behind the napkin she was using to wipe her mouth.

Josh pushed aside the empty platters and took a drink from his glass of sweet tea. "I'm glad we decided to share.

You would have missed out on the Voodoo and I'd have been jealous of those huge shrimp on the po'boy."

The server brought the bill and Josh snagged it from the woman's hand.

"No," Teri protested, "I'm supposed to cover the expenses. It's part of your publisher's budget."

"Not tonight," he said. "I chose the restaurant, I'll pay."

Once he'd reclaimed possession of his platinum card, Josh slid out of the booth and offered her his hand.

Accepting his assistance, she told him, "Thank you. I'm almost positive I wouldn't have been able to stand on my own."

"We'd better hurry," he said as they stepped outside. "It's five blocks back to Collingwood and it's about to rain."

Teri followed the direction of Josh's gaze and realized he was right. A huge black storm cloud was headed in their direction. Grateful for the fact she'd chosen a pair of flats rather than heels she took Josh's hand and followed him in a half-run, half-walk down the street.

By the time they arrived at Collingwood, the storm had started, lightly at first. Then, within five hundred feet of the front gate, the clouds opened up and dropped buckets of warm rain on top of them. Off in the distance, thunder rumbled and the first streaks of lightning broke across the dark sky. Laughing like two young children running through puddles, they made their way up the stairs and through the front door of the old home.

"Aren't you two a sight," Martha said when she met them in the hallway. "There are plenty of towels in the bathroom if you need them."

They made their way up to the third floor, still laughing, still brushing rain from their clothes.

Teri stopped at the door to her room and rummaged through her purse for the key. "I'd better get out of these wet clothes."

"Yeah, me too," Josh agreed. "I'll see you in the morning."

She let herself into her room and closed the door behind her, suddenly wishing for any excuse to extend her time with the professor.

Chapter 4

Josh stared at his computer screen, the light it shed the only illumination in the room. The power had gone out an hour earlier and, with the storm still raging, it wasn't likely to come back on until morning. Thank heaven he'd thought to charge his battery pack. Otherwise, he'd not have found the pictures and reports . . . information he'd only hoped existed.

He scrolled up and down the screen, checking and rechecking his find. The information, if correct, was extraordinary, although somewhat unbelievable. He opened his briefcase and removed the brown box belonging to Mrs. DeChambeau. Opening the smaller box inside, he withdrew the pink stone and held it up to the photo on the computer screen. The photograph was old, the contents blurred, but the size and shape were consistent.

Lost in his comparison, he barely heard the knock at his door. Slipping the stone into the front pocket of his jeans, he stood up from the desk. A second knock sounded, a bit louder this time, and he crossed the room and opened the door.

Teri stood on the threshold, a flashlight in her hand, its beam flickering and about to die.

"You wouldn't happen to have some spare batteries, would you? I went downstairs to find Martha but, apparently, she's gone to bed and I didn't want to disturb her."

"I'm not sure. Come on in and I'll look."

Teri stepped into his room and he closed the door behind her. "How's the research going?"

Josh had the sudden urge to share his findings, something he wouldn't ordinarily do with anyone but a trusted colleague. Yet, if he were right, just the idea of sounding it all out to another person seemed like the right thing to do.

"Actually, if you've got a minute, I've found something rather exciting regarding the elusive pink stone."

Rather than take a seat near the computer, Teri crossed the room and went to stand by the half-open window, most likely drawn there by the possibility of a cool breeze on a hot and muggy night. The storm lashed heavily against the top glass pane, thunder shook the building. A moment later, lightning lit up the sky, illuminating the grounds behind the old home.

As he expected, she turned from the window to face him. "Your room overlooks a cemetery."

"Yes, it does."

"And this is your *usual* room?" she confirmed, her tone filled with a mixture of surprise and disbelief.

"I find the old cemeteries of New Orleans fascinating. It might not be ancient Egyptian history, but its history all the same."

"Creepy history, maybe."

He weaved around the desk and antique settee until he stood at her side. The moon had slid from behind the dark clouds and sat like a spotlight in the sky.

"There, see that?" he said, pointing off in the distance. Teri turned in the direction he pointed, following his line of sight. "It's the crypt of one of the first voodoo priestesses to be buried here in the French Quarter."

"Like I said, creepy."

He chuckled. "And that one there," he said, pointing to a rather nondescript headstone, "is the grave of a two-year-old child who died of a simple infection in the late nineteenth century. The mix of graves and crypts and stories is, like I said, fascinating."

She spared one last glance at the graveyard then made her way to the desk. "I'll take your word for it." Motioning toward his laptop, she asked, "What have you found so far?"

Reminded of why he'd invited her to stay, Josh took his seat and tilted the screen in her direction.

"If I'm correct, the stone is called the *Eye of the Pharaoh* and belonged, originally, to Hatshepsut. She was the daughter of Tuthmosis I and longest reigning queen-Pharaoh of the eighteenth dynasty. After she died, she was buried alongside her father, and the stone was said to have been entombed with her as part of an ivory statue guarding her in the afterlife. However, legend has it, her stepson Tuthmosis III had the statue removed to be placed in his tomb when he died."

Josh pulled up the picture he'd been studying and then removed the stone from his pocket and held it up next to the article. "See," he said, motioning for her to move closer. "It's identical." He handed her the stone, their fingers brushing lightly in the transfer, the simple contact sending sparks of awareness across the back of his hand.

Teri took a seat on the arm of his chair and leaned over the desk. The soft scent of lilacs filled the space between them when she moved. Dressed in jeans and a soft cotton shirt, her long blond hair pulled back in a loose ponytail, she seemed even more relaxed than she had at the bookstore.

A familiar ache filled him, reminding him all-too-easily of his lack of physical contact, his career-driven celibacy.

"It does look similar," she agreed. "So, if this is the same stone, how did Dr. DeChambeau come to have it?"

"That's where the story gets interesting," he told her. "Or, as you might say, creepy."

"Creepier than a graveyard outside your bedroom window?"

"Yes, even creepier." Scrolling down the computer screen, he began recounting the unusual events surrounding the stone. "Apparently, Akhenaten, also known as Amenhotep

IV, had heard of the *Eye* and wanted the unusual stone for his wife, Queen Nefertiti, so he sent a group of three high priests and three soldiers in search of Tuthmosis III's burial site. The priests and soldiers found what they were looking for, but while on their way back to Akhenaten's temple, one by one, four of them were killed off in the most mysterious ways."

"Mysterious, how?" she asked.

"The first soldier was found with a stake through his heart, the second his throat slit. The first priest to die had his arms ripped off, the second priest lost his head. Pretty soon, the only two left were the high priest who was actually carrying the jewel and the last soldier believed to be the captain of the Pharaoh's guards."

"What happened to them?"

"Nobody knows. They never made it to their destination. Then, in 1922, a few months after Carter discovered Tutankhamen's tomb, another discovery was made. The bodies of two men and, in what was left of the robe one man wore, they found a pink stone. The stone was cataloged as part of the dig and brought back to the States."

"But what about eminent domain. Didn't the gemstone belong to Egypt?"

"Back then, there were no laws protecting archaeological discoveries. Between the legitimate scientists and the grave robbers, the country lost a lot of their artifacts to collectors of all kinds."

"That still doesn't explain what happened between 1922 and now and how Dr. DeChambeau ended up with the stone."

"That's where the story gets even more muddled. There were six men who took part in the 1922 expedition and, like the three soldiers and three priests, they suddenly began dying off once they'd returned to the States. The first three deaths were very violent. After the third death, one of the men made notes claiming the stone was cursed, protected by some unseen source from the underworld. He claimed he and the other two remaining men had decided to return the stone to Egypt and give it to the Museum of Antiquities in Cairo."

"And, did they?"

"Unfortunately, that's where the story ends. There's no mention of the three men or the stone after that point. The *Eye of the Pharaoh* never made it to Cairo, was never donated elsewhere and, as far as anyone knows, it never left the States."

"Dr. DeChambeau must have found it on one of his art buying trips," she reasoned.

"That was my conclusion as well. I'm just not sure where he found it."

"Does it matter?"

"For the sake of accuracy, it does. No archaeologist, or scholar of any discipline, wants to leave a story untold, especially one as cryptic as this."

His recounting of events complete, Teri stood and stepped away from the chair. She handed him back the pink stone and, as it had before, a warmth coursed through his body.

"It's getting late. I should go back to my room," she said.

"Yes, I suppose," he agreed, albeit reluctantly. "I've bent your ear long enough with these tales of Egyptian curses." He raised himself from the chair and crossed the room, tucking the stone back in the pocket of his jeans as he went. "Let me check the nightstand drawer for those batteries you wanted."

While she waited, Teri made her way back to the window. Was she suddenly as curious as he about the old cemetery and its inhabitants?

"Sorry," he said, coming to join her, "no batteries."

The moon had slipped back behind the clouds. The rain still pounded into the ground. The thunder and lightning, while farther away, still broke through from time to time.

"It's okay. I can find my way to the door by the light of your computer screen."

No sooner had she made the claim when the screen flickered, the low-battery warning blinking like a half-lit neon sign above a used car lot.

"Try to steer clear of the big chair," he teased, "I've already bruised my shin on it a couple of times."

She was about to step away, when a crash of thunder echoed around them, shaking the very foundation of the old building. Lightning rent the sky, hitting so close Teri jumped forward, landing against Josh's chest. Instinctively, he wrapped his arms around her and drew her into his embrace. When she looked up at him with wide, doe-like eyes, Josh lost any hope of resistance. He lowered his head and pressed his mouth to hers.

Her heart beat a wild tattoo against his chest, the rhythm echoing his own. The muggy night rolled in through the window, enclosing them in a cloak of perspiration.

He grasped her shoulders, intending to set her away. Yet, when she laid her hands against his chest, he couldn't stop himself from drawing her even closer, and willingly accepting a second, mind-boggling taste.

Teri closed her eyes and filled her senses with Josh's flavor, the sensual pull of his expert kiss. When he nipped at her lower lip, she gladly welcomed the slow, thorough invasion of his tongue.

Josh pressed her back against the window ledge and stepped closer, molding his hard angles to her curves. She knew she should say something and put a stop to what was happening between them. Yet, when he leaned into her and she felt the first brush of his arousal against her hip, it was all she could manage not to rub against him in wanton anticipation.

"Teri." His husky voice caressed her name. "Stop me, please."

She wrapped her arms around his neck and drew his mouth back to hers admitting, without words, she was powerless to grant his request.

He slid one hand beneath the hem of her shirt, dusting his fingertips across her middle, until he'd found her lace-covered breast. Slipping his hand beneath the edge of her bra, he cupped her gently in his grasp, and brushed his thumb across her nipple, drawing the docile center to life with no more than a few expert strokes.

She returned the invasion of his tongue with one of her own, drawing a groan from deep within his throat. He released her breast and placed both hands at her waist until he could lift her up and set her on the window ledge. Spreading her legs, he stepped between them until the firmest part of his body pressed against the neediest part of hers.

Josh captured her mouth in another deep, wet kiss. Teri stroked his tongue with her own, trading control of the kiss over and over until her head spun and her heart pounded.

With one hand, he pushed at the material of her shirt, slipping her arm from the sleeve. About to remove the opposite sleeve herself, she stopped suddenly when she heard the splintering of the window above her head and felt the first gust of wind against her back.

Josh fell backward, taking her with him, rolling them both out of the way of the flying shards. She glanced back over her shoulder. A gnarled tree branch had penetrated the empty pane and hung above them like so many crooked fingers. Were it not for Josh's quick reflexes, they would have both been showered in broken glass. He pulled her close and pressed her head to his shoulder, wrapping her tightly in his arms.

Then, as quickly as it had come, the raging wind ceased, the storm stilled and the room and everything around them went pitch black. Were it not for the heat of Josh's body pressed against her own, she wouldn't have even known he was there.

"Don't move," he whispered, his lips pressed to the pulse beating rapidly at the base of her throat. "Until we're sure it's over."

"I'm not going anywhere, even if I could see where anywhere was."

"That was one helluva kiss," he said, his laughter buried beneath the veil of her hair.

"I'd call it earth-shattering," she agreed.

They lay there a few moments longer, the mutual pounding of their hearts slowing down in time with their breathing. Josh took Teri's hand and pressed it against the floor. The carpet felt damp. So damp, in fact, it almost seemed as if they were lying on the ground instead of on a worn Persian rug.

"Something's not right," he said.

The ominous tone of his claim sent a shiver down her back. "I think the rain must have seeped in enough to ruin the carpet."

"That's not carpet, Teri. It's dirt."

Josh stood and drew her to her feet. Tentatively, they stepped forward, until they came to the closest wall.

"Take my hand," he instructed. "And, whatever you do, don't let go."

"No problem," she said, tightening her grip on his fingers.

He inched slowly forward, feeling his way along the wall. She pressed her free hand against the wall as well. Rather than the faded flocked wallpaper she expected, all she felt was cold, hard rock.

"Where are we?" she whispered.

"I'm not sure. I think we should follow this wall until we can find a way out."

Too frightened to disagree, Teri tightened her grasp on Josh's hand and moved when he moved. Within a few hundred feet, they came to a narrow opening. Josh stepped through, pulling her behind him. The passageway narrowed even more as they made their way forward.

"I can't see a thing," she said. "Talk about being caught between a rock and a hard place."

"If you thought things were creepy before, I'd venture they're a whole lot stranger now," Josh said, doing his best she suspected to lessen her fear with humor.

"There's some light," she said, pointing ahead.

"I see it."

Josh stopped just a few short of the end of the passageway, the light now bright enough to see where they were going. They ventured another twenty feet or so. Then, taking a firmer grip on her hand, he stepped out from between the rocks and onto a bed of sand, drawing her to his side.

"Where are we?" she asked.

Rather than respond, Josh grasped her shoulders and turned her around. She blinked once, twice, certain she'd fallen asleep and landed in the middle of some bizarre dream that included Josh and stone walls and sand.

"Well, for one thing we're in Egypt. And those, Miss Hunter," he said, pointing toward the horizon, "are the Great Pyramids of Giza."

Chapter 5

Wake up. Kick . . . to hell with it . . . just wake up!

She stretched out her hand and poked Josh in the chest, certain he was nothing more than a dream, an apparition. When her fingers met solid muscle, she told him, "Pinch me. I need to wake up."

"I'm not a figment of your imagination and you're not asleep." Withdrawing the pink stone from his pocket, he held it up to the waning sunlight. "Somehow, we've been brought here, and it must have something to do with this stone."

"You mean we've traveled halfway around the world by the power of a three-thousand-year-old, possibly cursed, jewel?"

"It would seem so, although I'm not quite ready to make such an outlandish assumption. At least not without a bit more research." He paused, turning full circle, stopping every so often to study their surroundings. "If I'm gauging the landscape correctly, we've not only traveled across miles, we've traveled through time."

She shook her head, unwilling to accept either possibility. "I'm as a big fan of H.G. Wells as the next person," she admitted, "but there's no such thing as time travel." When Josh didn't comment, she asked, "Is there?"

"Judging by the lack of formal roads leading away from the pyramids and the encampment just to the left of those rocks, I'd estimate we've arrived sometime in the early twentieth century."

She turned back to the passageway they'd just exited.

"So, if we go through there, we can get back to where we came from."

"Not likely. There has to be a catalyst, something to do with the *Eye* that brought us here."

"Yes, it's the curse," she said, unable to hide the trembling in her voice, "we're going to die because of a stupid rock."

Josh took a step in her direction and wrapped his arm around her shoulders, drawing her to his side. "If the curse were going to kill us, it would have done so either back in New Orleans when I first opened the box, or during our strange transport here to this place and time."

She leaned against the solid wall of Josh's chest and wrapped her arms around him. "I'm scared," she admitted. "I don't want to have my arms ripped off or lose my head."

"I don't believe we have anything to worry about. We're not trying to steal the stone. If anything we may have been brought here to return it to where it belongs."

"I suppose you know just where that would be?"

"I have my theories, as half-baked as they may be."

"Half-baked is better than raw," she suggested.

"I doubt the curse would have been set in place by Tuthmosis III. After all, he, too, died not long after removing the statue from his stepmother's tomb. My guess is we need to return the stone to Hatshepsut, queen-Pharaoh and rightful owner of the *Eye*."

"And, of course, you also know how we're going to accomplish this feat."

"I haven't got all the logistics figured out as yet, but at least I know where to start."

"And where would that be?" she asked, wary of any plan involving curses and tombs.

Josh pointed toward a group of tents off in the distance. "There. Someone's out here on an expedition. We need to find out who they are and what they're hoping to find."

"How will that help?"

"It will allow me to pinpoint the exact month and year and tell me whether Hatshepsut's tomb has already been discovered, or if we'll have to find it ourselves."

"We're going to go looking for a tomb?"

"The tomb was originally discovered by British archaeologist Howard Carter in 1902, but there was no indication it was the tomb of a noble so it was never properly excavated."

"But I thought she was a queen."

"After her father died Hatshepsut married her half-brother Tuthmosis II. When her husband/brother died, she ruled on behalf of his infant son Tuthmosis III. After Hatshepsut's death, Tuthmosis III, in addition to removing the statue, took steps to erase all traces of her in order to remove the female interruption in the male Tuthmosis lineage, including the falsification of the inscriptions on her sarcophagus and tomb. Carter came back later, in 1920, and removed two empty sarcophagi, a number of canopic jars and some gilded boxes which he took to the museum, still believing the tomb belonged to servants rather than nobility. Positive identification of Hatshepsut's remains didn't occur until the late 1980s."

"So then, depending on the year, we'll either find what we're looking for in the museum or in the stepson's tomb," she guessed.

"Not exactly. Tuthmosis III's tomb was actually discovered much earlier and cleaned out of most of its valuables by grave robbers. Somewhere around the end of the nineteenth century, Victor Loret cleared the remainder of the tomb and cataloged where everything might have been. Of course, according to the legend, the stone had long since been removed by the priests and soldiers, thereby causing the supposed curse."

Josh took her hand and started walking toward the encampment.

"What are we searching for then?" she asked. "And do you know where to look?"

"I'm pretty sure we need to find the ivory statue, assuming it was taken later by the grave robbers or as part of the excavation, rather than by the priests and guards. If we reunite the statue and the stone, we may be able to stave off the curse long enough to return everything to Hatshepsut."

"I like the sound of ending the curse," she admitted.

"I have a general idea of where we'll need to start. However, it would a lot easier if I had my laptop or the university's database."

"Darn, I knew I shouldn't have left my PDA in the hotel room," she joked, hoping to both lighten the moment and lessen her fear of the unknown.

Rather than respond to her lighthearted attempt, Josh tightened his grip on her hand and picked up his speed. "We'd better get to the camp before the sun sets. The temperature will drop fast and the winds pick up even faster. At the moment, shelter is our first priority."

"How will we explain our sudden appearance in the middle of nowhere?"

"I'm not sure yet, but I'll think of something before we get there. You just follow my lead, whatever it is."

Josh wound his way through the myriad of tents, Teri following closely at his heels. They passed a group of diggers huddled around a campfire, gladly partaking in a meal of bread, dried meat, fruit, and wine. The acrid smell of hashish assaulted his senses and he quickened his steps, pulling a curious Teri after him. When they finally made their way to the middle of the compound, they found the largest structure, no doubt the tent of the group's leader. Off to the side he noticed an early 1920s auto and a truck with wooden side rails.

They approached the man mostly likely in charge. "Hello there," Josh greeted. "We were hoping to speak to the head archaeologist."

A man who looked to be in his mid-sixties turned in their direction. "I'm Henry Sutton, University of Edinburgh, and this is my expedition." Shading his eyes from the low hanging sun, he asked, "Who might you two be?"

"Professor Joshua Cain, Princeton University, and this is my wife, Teri."

He felt the squeeze of Teri's hand, his introduction as his wife obviously taking her by surprise.

"A Yank, and a bloody Princeton one at that," Sutton said, his Cockney accent unmistakable. "And pray tell, Joshua Cain, what are the two of you doing out here in the middle of the desert, with no mode of transport in sight?"

"We came out with a colleague to scout for a vacant site. We'd found what I thought to be a perfect spot, but my colleague disagreed. We argued and he took off in our auto, taking all of our belongings with him. We waited awhile for him to cool off and come back. When he didn't, we thought we'd better seek shelter before nightfall."

"A smart idea." Sutton swept his arm wide to encompass the entire camp. "However, as you can see, we're pretty full up."

"We'd be grateful for anything, even a spot in your supply tent."

Sutton gave them a quick up-and-down appraisal. "How do I know, for sure, you're who you say you are?"

Josh raised and lowered his shoulders in an attempt at a nonchalant shrug. "You can ask me anything you like."

"Who was the last of your lot to man a successful dig?"

Josh closed his eyes and prayed he'd gauged the time

period correctly. His mind whirled through the university's vast historical directory. "Professor Pemberton was the last sanctioned expedition in 1919. There've been a few stragglers since then, but nothing official." He paused. "My direct report, Charles Engleworth, can verify my sabbatical if you'd like to send him a telegram."

Again, Sutton gave them the once-over. "I suppose we could arrange a tent at the edge of the camp. Our driver won't be going into Cairo until day after tomorrow, but you're welcome to ride with him then."

Josh offered up some additional insight. "I'm fully accredited through both the university and the Egyptian government. I'd be happy to work off the cost of our room and a meal or two, if you're willing. I can help with the dig, or assist in cataloging."

"How do I know you won't run off with anything you find?"

"You have my word."

"The word of a Yank," Sutton said, laughing. "I'll see what I can find for you and your wife to do around here until the truck leaves. In the meantime, I'll have one of my men snag you a tent and some blankets from the supplies. You can set up there," he said, pointing toward the far side of the compound. "I don't suppose you've got something more fitting to work in than those denim trousers. They're not very practical in the heat of the day."

Josh glanced down at his jeans and back up at Sutton. "We hadn't expected to be doing any digging today, only looking. I should be okay. It wouldn't be the first time I'd been on a dig dressed this way."

"Suit yourself," Sutton said, giving a shrug of his shoulders. "If you change your mind, though, there may be some extra khaki camp pants in among the supplies."

"Thank you for the shelter," Josh said. "And, should you

give the go-ahead, the opportunity to work off our debt."

They were about to head in the direction Sutton had indicated when his question stopped them in their tracks. "Mrs. Cain, do you teach at Princeton too?"

When Teri turned to face Sutton, Josh held his breath in anticipation of her response.

"No, not me. I'm just the wife of a very poorly paid professor. If I had my choice in the matter, I'd be back in New Jersey having tea with the other professors' wives."

Henry Sutton nodded in appreciation of her honest answer. "Well, Mrs. Cain, I might have something you can help me with, assuming I allow your husband out on my dig."

Instinctively, Josh drew Teri close to his side, the simple action drawing Sutton's laughter yet again.

"Not to worry, Cain," he said, "I wasn't making a pass at your woman." Closing the distance between himself and where they stood, the older man laid his hand on Josh's shoulder and added, "Take my word for it, you're far more to my liking than your beautiful wife."

"Your wife?" Teri said softly, as they walked toward the edge of the encampment.

"It'll be much safer for you if they think we're married. There aren't too many single women out in the middle of the desert. However, these men do respect property, ownership. You'll be off-limits as long as they think you belong to me."

"Property? I'm not your property, Dr. Cain."

He shot her a quick glance, a half-grin, half-leer. "I know that, you know that, but this is not the twenty-first century, Teri. These men have no clue what's in store for them with the feminist movement. And again, for your safety, I'd suggested you let it stay that way."

Teri stood inside the hastily constructed tent, her head nearly touching the top, the enclosure so cramped she could stretch out her arms and reach the sides. Josh had made a single pallet out of two thick woolen blankets in the corner and set up a stool and wash basin near the front flap.

Home sweet home, and one very narrow bed.

Washing her hands and face with water from the basin, she used a cotton hand towel to pat herself dry. She'd barely set the cloth aside when Josh entered the tent carrying two canteens and a basket filled with dried meat, nuts, and fruit.

"I'm sorry about the cramped accommodations," he said immediately.

"It's all right. Given our unusual circumstances, this tent is the least of our worries."

He took a seat at the foot of their makeshift bed and motioned for her to join him. She sat as well, her back to the wall of the tent, the basket of food between them.

"Listen, Teri, about what happened, almost happened, back in my room," he began, "I don't think we should get any further involved while we're here. The last thing we need is to lose focus on what we're here for and getting back to where we belong. A physical relationship would complicate matters."

"I agree."

"We will need to share close quarters, both for appearances and practicality."

"Yes, of course." She met his serious gaze and forced a smile to her lips. "I understand completely."

"I promise you, we will get out of this and go home."

"I believe you, and I trust you, Josh. If there's anything I can do to help, all you have to do is ask."

"I'm sure I'll need your help along the way. In the meantime, though, just pretending to be a lowly-paid professor's wife is a good start." He paused for a moment, tilted his head, and repeated, "Lowly paid?"

"Back in the early twentieth century, I'd bet salaries aren't nearly as cushy as they are now."

Josh chuckled. "You're definitely right about the 1920s. However, they're not *that* cushy now either."

"So, what did you bring to eat? I'm starved."

He handed her a bunch of grapes and a strip of cured beef. "Hopefully, you don't mind warm food."

Their meal complete, Josh set the basket aside and turned back the top blanket on the bed.

"I also brought a couple of lightweight cotton shirts from the supply tent," he told her. "You might find them a bit more comfortable to sleep in than your clothes."

"Yes, I suppose I would."

When she hesitated, he stood and handed her one of the gauzy shirts. "I'll wait outside for you to change. Don't take too long, though, the wind's starting to pick up."

As quickly as she could, she slipped out of her shoes, socks, jeans, tee shirt, and bra then donned the shirt over her skimpy lace panties. After folding her discarded clothes into a neat pile, she slipped between the blankets just as Josh re-entered the tent.

Obviously not shy, Josh stripped out of his shoes, jeans, and shirt and came to join her wearing only his boxers and socks.

Outside the tent, the wind increased, just as Josh had said it would, the temperature dropping as well. When Josh drew her into his arms and pillowed her head on his shoulder, Teri closed her eyes and welcomed the security of his embrace.

About to drift off to sleep, one final thought crept into her head.

"Josh?"

"Hmm," he mumbled, obviously already breaching the edge of slumber.

"If the *Eye of the Pharaoh* is truly what brought us here and we return it to where it belongs, how will we get home?"

He sighed deeply, his warm breath washing over her. "I'm not sure," he admitted. "I have to trust that whomever, or whatever, brought us here will know how to send us back."

When she awoke the next morning, Josh was already up and dressed and standing outside their tent talking to one of the diggers.

She sat up, pushed her hair out of her eyes, and reached for the nearby canteen. The sun had likely been up for less than an hour and already the temperature was climbing rapidly. The dust, kicked up by the previous night's wind, clung to the mesh walls of the tent, making her grateful for their shelter, no matter how cramped and intimate.

If she closed her eyes, memories of earlier that morning came back to her in a rush, the moments just before dawn when she'd awoke to the imprint of Josh's erection pressed against her hip, the weight of his hand lying against her waist, the thin barrier of the cotton shirt doing little to shield her from the heat of his bare skin everywhere their bodies touched.

She'd thought about rolling onto her back, of removing the temptation his arousal generated within her. Yet, in the end, she'd only closed her eyes, accepted the tingling sensations coursing through her body, and fallen back asleep, certain of only two things.

First, there would be no way to avoid the inevitable physical encounter, and, second, she wasn't sure how much longer she could wait.

Chapter 6

"Good morning, Mrs. Cain. I trust you slept well." Henry Sutton stood as she approached, extending his hand in greeting. "I'll have my man pour you a cup of coffee and bring some fruit and bread."

"Thank you," she responded. "And thank you for allowing my husband to help out with the dig." Taking a seat across from Sutton, she added, "I know he would be absolutely bored to tears if he had nothing to do."

"Don't think I didn't test his knowledge. He's got some wonderful insight about excavation. And, it's always good to have another set of trained hands to help with the work. Assuming, of course, the person helping doesn't have an ulterior motive."

"I assure you, Mr. Sutton, Josh's intentions are pure."

"I've been around long enough to know Egypt and all of its undiscovered riches have a way making even the most honorable man greedy, Mrs. Cain."

"Not Josh," she assured him. "His motives for helping are purely academic. He wants nothing more than to lend a hand until we're able to return to Cairo."

"As I mentioned last evening," Sutton began, "I have something you could help with as well if you'd be interested in keeping busy."

"Yes, I would definitely be interested. I'm not as knowledgeable as my husband, but I also don't want to sit around and do nothing." Taking a sip of the strong coffee placed in front of her, she asked, "What is it you need me to do?"

"Each day, after the items have been brought above ground, we sort through them by size, significance, and perceived value. Then, each item is listed in our inventory book and boxed up for transport. As you can imagine, the cataloguing can become quite time consuming."

"I'd be happy to help in any way I can," she told him. The idea of viewing newly found artifacts piqued her interest, because of both the history and the chance to learn more about Josh's love for archaeology.

After they'd finished their coffee and morning meal, she eagerly followed Henry Sutton into the tent in the middle of the compound. One area was cordoned off to the side for what she suspected were the man's living quarters. Along the walls of the tent, long, rectangular tables were covered with dirt-encrusted pieces of history. Under the tables were brown boxes waiting to be filled. In the middle of everything sat a square table, two chairs, and a stack of ledgers and basket filled with various types of marking devices.

"What I'd like your help with is cataloging and boxing the items from yesterday's dig. I'll examine every piece and then bring it to you. You'll enter the description, as I give it to you, into the inventory. Then, you'll select a box big enough to hold the piece, and write the corresponding inventory number on the top of the box."

"That sounds easy enough."

"Once you've selected and labeled the box, I'll add the proper packing material, seal the box, and put my individual mark on the outside."

"Your mark?" she asked. "Josh has never mentioned anything about a 'mark' to me." With any luck, her comment would appear innocent rather than prying.

"Every archaeologist creates themselves an identifiable design, a mark. That way, if there is ever a question as to who found and packaged the archaeological find the mark is proof positive of ownership."

"But couldn't someone else claim the mark as their own?"

"Before we come out on a dig, we register our marks with the Museum of Antiquities in Cairo. I've used the same mark for nearly ten years now and never had a problem."

Did Josh also have a mark exclusive to his work? Or, had more modern times developed better ways to claim the right of discovery?

"If you're ready, we'll start with some of the smaller pieces," Sutton suggested.

Her hands literally itched with the thought of touching the priceless antiquities. Nodding, she said, "I'm ready, whenever you are."

Henry Sutton brought over a limestone relief, no larger than a cell phone yet, even buried beneath thousands of years of dirt, she could make out the exquisite detail of the piece. Laying the relief down on a soft cloth in the center of the table, Sutton opened the book and handed her an old-fashioned fountain pen.

She turned the logbook to the next page, and waited for instructions.

"Item one-forty," Sutton began, motioning toward the next line on the page. "Limestone tablet, circa 1585 BCE, chipped corner."

She transcribed the information on line one-forty and then went to retrieve a box big enough to secure the tablet. The moment she lifted the box into her hands, she realized it was the same type that had held the mysterious pink stone.

"Is this box sufficient?" she asked, returning to the table.

"Yes, that will be perfect." Pointing to the corner of the box, he instructed, "Write down the book number, followed by a dash and then the line number. Once you've labeled the box, set the limestone in it very carefully and move it to the center table."

"When do you finish packing the items?"

"I usually wait until there are a dozen or so before I start stuffing and sealing the boxes. Once they're sealed and my mark added, we move them to the back shelves."

"Who usually helps you?" she asked, curious as to why she'd been entrusted with such an important job.

"Kevin, my second in charge," he told her. "Today, he's down on the dig with your husband."

She let Sutton's words sink in, his subtle admission of wariness. To parody another of her favorite sayings, *Keep your friends close and strangers closer*. Obviously, they were being watched. She worried about the safety of the pink stone. What if Sutton thought they'd found it here, on his dig, rather than brought it with them? She'd have to share her concerns with Josh the minute he came above ground.

The next item Sutton brought for cataloging was an urn. "Item one-forty-one," he dictated. "Clay urn, circa 1585 BCE, painted edges."

"It seems to be in remarkable shape for something made of clay," she thought aloud.

"Likely this vessel was used to store olive oil or some other seasoning and was rarely used other than during meals," Sutton explained. "I'm sure we'll have piles upon piles of shards of similar pieces that didn't weather the passing of time quite as well as this."

She and Sutton worked straight through until the midday meal, stopping only when Josh and the others came up to eat. Although she wanted a moment of privacy to relay her concerns to Josh, she could see he was in demand, his obvious expertise drawing admiration from both Sutton and his crew.

The men sat around the center table and ate heartily, replenishing their strength for the rigors of the excavation. Josh glanced her way on a couple of occasions, his half-smile telling her without words, how important this conversation was toward gaining Sutton's trust. She sat on the opposite side of the table and listened closely, eager to soak up as much information as she could.

"Dr. Cain, I understand you found a possible opening to yet another chamber," Sutton said.

"It looks promising," Josh confirmed. "However, until I've cleared away the encrusted dirt, I wouldn't want to jump to conclusions. It could be an unsuccessful attempt for ventilation, or maybe even a trap."

"A trap?" Sutton asked.

"There have been reports of late coming from some of the digs in the Valley of the Kings, of booby-trapped tombs, supposedly designed that way to protect the inhabitants of the chamber. Fortunately, once the traps have been disabled and the chambers breached, the results have been remarkable."

"Then I say let's be as careful as need be, Dr. Cain," Sutton agreed. "But, by all means, let's do our best to get to the other side of that wall."

"So, Mrs. Cain," Josh teased when he entered their tent, "how was your day?"

"Very busy, Dr. Cain," she told him. "How about yours?"

Josh tossed aside his sweat-stained shirt and stepped out of his jeans, leaving him in standing there in his underwear. Walking to the rear of the tent, he poured water into the chipped basin and lifted a handful to his face.

When he raised his head, he told her, "Hot, dirty, but otherwise exhilarating as always. Excavation techniques and locations I'd only read about in textbooks are now at my fingertips. As unsettling as our predicament is, I have to admit, I'm enjoying myself immensely."

When he stretched his arms above his head and twisted in an effort to work out the kinks in his muscles, she did her best not to stare. Josh had a magnificent physique. He was definitely not a skinny, bookworm-ish professor.

"Did you find anything interesting?" she asked. Hopefully a conversation would derail her lust-filled thoughts.

"One or two significant pieces, but not much else."

"What about the new chamber you mentioned at lunch?"

"It turned out to be a false wall, much as I'd expected."

"I'm sure Sutton was disappointed."

"Not as much as you would have thought. He seems to be quite knowledgeable and understands that nothing, short of full discovery, is a given."

"Were you able to identify the occupant of the tomb?" she asked.

"By my estimation, we're excavating the tomb of a seventeenth dynasty high priest. However, there are indications of grave robbing going back as far as the time of Ramesses III. I did discover a gold trimmed water vessel, though, which leads me to believe if they move the search over a few hundred feet, they may find another chamber."

"Are you going to tell them that?"

The expression on Josh's face was almost comical. "Not unless I have to," he admitted. "I figure, if they're not smart enough to find it on their own, too bad for them."

"What happened to the vessel you found?" she asked.

"I gave it to Professor March."

"Professor March?"

"Sutton's assistant, Kevin March."

"Oh yes, your watchdog."

Josh chuckled. "It would seem they want me for my expertise, but they don't trust me." Pausing to dry his face and arms, he asked, "So, what did you do today?"

"I helped enter the pieces they'd already found into inventory and box them up for transport."

"Under Sutton's watchful eye, I presume."

"He never left me for a minute."

"Well, at least you didn't get strip-searched."

"Strip searched?" She couldn't hide her surprise. The idea of Josh being searched reminded her of her earlier concern for the stone.

"Yes. It's common practice to make sure the diggers aren't keeping a little for themselves."

"What about the stone? How did you hide that?"

"I didn't," he said simply. "You did."

"I don't understand."

"Check the watch pocket in your jeans."

She did as he instructed, tucking her fingertips into the slim pocket. Sure enough, the stone rested solidly along the bottom seam.

"What if they'd wanted to search me too? After all, I did work around their inventory all day."

Josh took her hand and twirled her around in front of him, his gaze running over her from head to toe, coming to rest at last on her face. Beneath the soft cotton of her shirt, she could feel her heart beating rapidly. If she measured her pulse no doubt it would have doubled in pace.

"By the fit of those jeans, I'm pretty sure they would have noticed if you'd tried to heist an urn or a painted relief."

She turned away from him, pretending to busy herself with straightening a blanket that didn't need fixing. "Speaking of jeans," she said, "if you can find something else to wear, I'd be happy to wash yours for you and hang them out to dry."

"Ah, Mrs. Cain, ever the dutiful wife," he joked. "I took Sutton's advice and grabbed a pair of camp pants from the supply tent. I hung them on the tent rope to air out a bit. Chances are they're not much cleaner than my jeans."

"Even though you had the more exciting adventure today, I did make a discovery of my own," she told him.

"What type of discovery?"

"The brown box the stone came in is identical to the boxes Professor Sutton uses to ship his artifacts. And, he uses a numbering system similar to the one faded out on Dr. DeChambeau's box."

"And the strange hieroglyphic?" Josh asked.

"I couldn't remember what the mark on the original box looked like, but Sutton's symbol resembles a long neck bird."

"I'd have to get a look at it to see if it's the same. If the research was right, the stone isn't scheduled for discovery for another few months, so it likely wasn't found at this site."

"Since we have the stone, whomever makes the discovery will only recover the remains of the priest and guard, right?"

Josh shrugged. "I'm guessing so. After all, they can't find something we have in our possession."

"I'm starving. I don't suppose you'd like to treat your wife to dinner, would you?"

"It would be my pleasure." Nodding toward the front of the tent, he added, "Assuming you could hand me some pants to wear."

They filled their plates and then joined their hosts at the table just outside the main tent. Both men were engaged in conversation on the opposite side of where she and Josh sat and she strained to hear what they were saying.

"I was just telling Kevin," Sutton began, his attention turned toward where Josh sat, "you probably found the most valuable piece so far on this dig. We appreciate it."

"I got lucky," Josh said simply.

"We've been discussing it and wonder if you and your lovely wife would like to stay on for a while longer. We could use someone with your knowledge. And, I have to admit, Mrs. Cain was a god-send today with the inventory."

"Teri told me you have quite an impressive set up. I'd love to take a look at it." Josh paused, adding, "As for staying on, we're honored to be asked. However, our first priority is tracking down our belongings, not to mention our travel papers."

Sutton frowned, disappointment spreading across his weathered face. "I can understand your concern. Perhaps, once you've completed your business in Cairo, you could return. We could write up a partnership agreement regarding any valuable discoveries."

"We'll certainly give your offer serious consideration," Josh told him.

After dinner, Teri returned to their tent, one of Sutton's workers following behind her with a bucket of water and some hand-shaved soap. And, much to her delight, an old-fashioned scrub board.

"Thank you," she said when he set the items down at the opening of their tent.

The man nodded, bowed, and scurried away, leaving her to launder their clothes and hang them up to dry.

Seated on a folding camp chair in front of their tent, she stood when Josh approached. He'd been conversing with Sutton and his group for over an hour and she was curious about what he'd discovered. "Did you get a look at the boxes?" she asked.

"Yes. I don't believe it's the same design. I tried to picture how it would look faded, as it was on DeChambeau's box. The characteristics were different. In all likelihood, someone other than Sutton and his partner are going to be the ones to find the remains of the high priest and Pharaoh's guard."

Teri pulled back the tent flap and went inside. "You coming in?" she asked when Josh didn't follow.

"I thought I'd give you a few minutes to get ready for bed."

She spared a fleeting thought for her undergarments drying on the makeshift clothesline next to Josh's jeans and shirt. Stepping back outside the tent, she snagged her panties off the line and went back inside.

Through the thin mesh wall, she heard Josh's laughter.

"What's so funny?" she asked, loud enough for him to hear.

"It's a miracle those were still here."

"Why would anyone want my panties? We're in a camp full of men."

Rather than respond, he laughed all the louder.

Josh rolled over on the woolen pallet until he faced away from the temptation of Teri's warm, inviting curves. What he wouldn't give for the chance to take her into his arms and make love to her until the sun rose over the pyramids. He sighed deeply, willing his erection away, reverting to silently reciting the entire eighteenth, nineteenth, and twentieth dynasties to himself, including the years of their reigns and a listing of their many consorts, in an effort to control his unruly body.

Unfortunately, his body had a mind of its own.

About to climb out of bed and go for a walk, he stopped suddenly when Teri rolled over and wrapped her arm around his waist, her delicate hand falling against his stomach. If he moved even the slightest, she'd have herself a handful of horny man.

"Josh," she said softly, her breath wafting against his shoulder.

"Yes?"

"How long before the sun comes up?"

"An hour, maybe a bit more. Why?"

A shiver skated the length of his spine when she slid her hand down his body and enclosed his arousal in her grasp.

"Since we're both awake, I thought maybe we could find something interesting to do."

Chapter 7

"Teri," he whispered, her name coming out on a hiss as he sucked in a deep draft of air.

She pictured him gritting his teeth then moved her hand once, twice, sliding her palm along the surface of his erection. His breath caught.

"If you truly believe we'll be able to spend another night, even another two hours, lying next to each other without touching, without this . . ." To emphasize her point, she brushed her hand over him again, measuring him, caressing him. "Then you're as foolish as those men who can't find the right place to dig."

"It's not that I don't want to. I do, I definitely do." He covered her hand with his, stilling the progress she knew was driving him insane. "We can't be distracted in our purpose for being here."

"Is there something we could be doing, at this very moment, to find the statue?"

"No, not at the moment," he admitted.

"Good."

Sliding atop him, she straddled his hips, and sat back on her heels. Reaching for the hem of the shirt she wore, she pulled it over her head and tossed it aside. When he raised his hands and cupped her breasts, she closed her eyes and released a long sigh.

"I can't protect you." Even as he uttered the words, he was pulling her to him for a long, deep kiss.

"I don't need protecting, Dr. Cain," she told him when the thoroughly delicious kiss ended. She scrambled from the woolen pallet, stood at the foot of their bed, and slid her panties down her legs. Leaning forward, she tugged at the waistband of his boxers, drawing them down his legs until they were both naked.

When she lay down beside him, Josh rolled onto his side and drew her into his embrace. Slowly, he kissed her cheeks, her eyelids, her throat, and finally her lips. He caressed her breasts, skimmed his fingertips along her midriff, then across the plane of her belly. She squirmed beneath Josh's gentle touch, wanting more, needing a firmer touch.

Boldly, she grasped his hand in hers and slid it down her body until he could cup the part of her aching for his touch. Josh pressed his mouth to hers, nipped at her lip until she opened for him, and then slid his tongue inside. In time with the rhythm of their kiss, she welcomed the intrusion of his fingers deep within her aroused body.

Her hips rose and fell in time with the stroke of Josh's hand, each push of his fingers deeper than the last. One stroke, ten, until her body convulsed in an orgasm so strong it nearly took her breath away. An orgasm that went on and on until she felt as she were melting from the inside out.

She'd barely recouped when he rolled on top of her and filled her completely. He began slowly, re-stoking the embers of the fire within her body, gradually picking up his speed until Teri could feel the first wave of a new, stronger climax coming on.

She grasped his hips in her hands, pulling him forward, demanding he succumb to the pressure as easily as she. Josh rose up on his hands and drove into her over and over until she could sense his eminent release. Closing her eyes, she let a wave of contentment wash over her, through her, knowing

Josh was going over the edge with her and they were both falling headfirst into the hot Egyptian sunrise.

As always, the morning was filled with a flurry of activity. Supplies were checked, ropes and heavy tools inspected for stability, canteens filled with water, and plans outlined for where each digger and each overseer would work.

"What's your plan for today, Josh?" Sutton asked.

"I'm not certain yet. However, the discovery of the false wall yesterday leads me to believe it was only a decoy. I'd like to concentrate on the opposite wall, scrape away some of the dirt, and see if it's possible there could still be a third chamber."

"Take one of the diggers to assist you," Kevin March told him. "I can make do with one less."

"I'd appreciate that," Josh confirmed, "especially if there are blocks of stone to be moved."

When the group left for the early morning excavation, Sutton and Teri returned to the main tent, another half-dozen items ready for cataloging and packing.

"If your husband is right, Mrs. Cain, this dig could turn out to be very profitable."

"By the look of all these boxes, I'd say you've already found a sizeable return on your investment of time and money."

"Not everything is as well preserved as the piece Josh found yesterday," Sutton admitted. "That's one reason we'd like to have him stay. As knowledgeable and experienced as both Kevin and I are, your husband seems to have an almost uncanny ability to see beyond the obvious."

"He is very gifted," she said. "And, back at Princeton, he's considered the utmost authority in his field."

"I've no doubt of that, Mrs. Cain, no doubt at all." He paused and then added, "I do find it strange though that our paths have never crossed. Surely this is not his first trip to Egypt."

She shrugged. "No, of course not. However, we haven't been married all that long, Professor. I'm honestly not sure when he was here last." Mentally, she made herself a note to fill Josh in on what she'd told Sutton.

Piece by piece, Sutton delivered each item to the table where she worked, dictated the entry for the logbook, and then entrusted her with selecting the correct box for packaging. The first piece, a limestone stele was breathtaking in its intricacy, the etching depicting a family of four as well an assortment of animals. Safely tucked into the box she'd selected, she pushed the work of art aside.

"This is beautiful," she commented, lifting the next piece in her hand.

"Despite being no more than a couple inches in diameter, this scarab is very detailed," Sutton confirmed. "And, likely worth twice as much as some of the pieces ten times its size."

They worked in silence, moving from one find to the next. "Is there anything else I can do to help?" she asked once she'd boxed the final item.

"No, thank you. That was the last piece for cataloging. I've two more boxes to pack and then we'll be done until the men return from the site. We've had a very productive morning."

They'd barely completed their work when a loud rumble echoed around them. Beneath their feet, the ground shook violently.

"What was that?" she asked. "What's happening?"

Sutton raced to the front of the tent, Teri close at his heels.

"That, Mrs. Cain, is the last noise an archaeologist ever wants to hear. It's the sound of a collapsing site."

Teri paced the ground above the excavation site, anxiously awaiting Josh's arrival topside. Sutton stood off to the side, his gaze trained on the narrow opening leading to the dig. Word had arrived just moments before of the collapse of one wall and, as yet, only a few of Sutton's workers had come up from below.

"What's going on?" Sutton asked the first of the men to reach them.

"I'm not sure, Professor. I know we lost one of the diggers beneath a fallen chunk of limestone. Kevin and Dr. Cain are assisting in extracting him from beneath the slab."

"They're both okay, then?" she asked, relief washing through her at lightning speed.

"As far as I could tell," the young man said. "Professor March wouldn't let anyone on the other side of the wall."

"You go get cleaned up," Sutton told him, "and make sure the scrape on your arm gets looked at right away."

"Yes sir." He did as instructed, hurrying toward the medical tent, anxious, she suspected, to be as far away from danger as possible.

Teri resumed her pacing certain she'd covered at least a dozen miles in the past half hour. Three more of Sutton's students came above ground, followed by a handful of dust-covered diggers. Much to her dismay, none of them could give an update on what was happening below.

As if he could sense her worry, Sutton said, "If they're not up in the next thirty minutes, I'll go down myself and look for them."

"I'll go with you," she said.

"No, you'll stay here. A dig, especially one as fragile as this is no place for an amateur."

She wanted to argue, yet she had to admit he was right. If anything, she'd be of little or no help and, more than likely, be in the way.

Twenty minutes passed with no one else emerging from the dig. The sun lingered on the horizon mere moments from setting. Soon it would be dark. Another wave of concern washed over her.

Sutton started toward the entryway leading underground, when suddenly the shadowy figures of two men appeared, a canvas litter suspended between them. The moment Josh and Kevin March set the digger's body down, she rushed forward and threw herself into Josh's open arms.

"Thank goodness," she whispered against his chest, burying her face against his shoulder. "I was so worried."

Josh wrapped his arms around her and pulled her tight against his body. When she looked up into his eyes, he lowered his head and pressed his mouth to hers.

She felt the slide of Josh's hands across her bottom. Against her throat, he whispered, "Don't sit down anywhere or turn your back on Sutton."

It was then she realized Josh had slipped something into the back pocket of her jeans. He was about to set her away when she drew him back to her chest and held on for dear life. Josh tightened his embrace, as if he could tell her actions were relief motivated, not meant as a show for the others. She could feel the pounding of Josh's heartbeat as surely as she felt her own.

Once she stepped back and Josh released her, she tugged at her rumpled tee shirt and drew it down over her hips as discreetly as she could, mindful of Josh's words to protect whatever he'd slipped into the pocket of her jeans.

"We were worried about the two of you," Sutton said, coming up to slap Josh on the back before walking over and putting his arms around his partner's shoulders and drawing him into an embrace.

"If it hadn't been for Dr. Cain," Kevin said, stepping out of Sutton's arms, "we'd have lost more than one man." Drawing a deep breath, he continued. "The wall started to crumble. We actually heard it before we saw anything. Josh rushed everyone out of the catacomb, but the one digger caught his foot on a jagged rock and fell. We both tried to get to him, but it was too late."

Sutton's cheeks grew red and his hand trembled where it still lay against Kevin March's arm. "You should have both come back up right away."

Josh gave an adamant shake his head. "We couldn't leave the man behind to be buried completely if the wall gave way a second time."

"And, if it had, you'd have both gone with him," Sutton pointed out, the wisdom of his words sinking in for her, if not for Josh.

"Well we didn't," Josh pointed out. "And now the man's family can bury him properly."

Sutton motioned for two of the other diggers to come and remove the man's body before turning to survey the opening to the site.

"Not meaning to sound crass given the unfortunate circumstances," Sutton said, "but what's left of the site?"

"Actually," Kevin began, "once the dust settles and it's safe to go back inside, we may have found another chamber." Nodding in Josh's direction, he clarified, "Or, should I say, Dr. Cain found another chamber."

The four of them started down the embankment toward the camp. When Josh took her hand in his, she gladly accepted the warmth of his grasp.

"This is why you need to join our expedition," Sutton commented as they walked, "Together we could discover the next big piece of archaeological history."

"Like I said," Josh reminded him, "we'll take your offer under serious consideration."

The moment they stepped into the privacy of their tent, Josh took her into his arms. She was about to raise her mouth to his for a kiss, when she realized he was only retrieving the item he'd hidden on her person.

"I thought you weren't going to show them the chamber,"

she said, extremely disappointed when he turned away from her and toward the kerosene lamp in the corner of the tent.

"There was nothing left to find in the original site and I decided we needed a stake for when we arrive in Cairo."

"A stake?"

"Who knows how long returning the stone is going to take. We'll have to have something to live on."

"What did you find?" she asked, joining him beside the lamp.

"This."

He held up a beautiful gold-encrusted relief with etching on each edge. The piece was far more ornate than the one she'd cataloged on their first day. The size of man's wallet, the dirt-covered artifact would surely cover their costs, assuming they could find someone to buy the piece.

"Where will you sell it?"

"I can't take it to the museum, since we were scavenging on someone else's site. However, I'm confident I can find a black market buyer for the piece."

"That sounds dangerous."

"More dangerous than being three-thousand years and five-thousand miles from home?" he asked.

"No, I guess not," she agreed.

"Now, we just have to find a way to keep this hidden until the truck leaves for Cairo tomorrow afternoon."

"If you can find some soft cloth for me to cut into strips, I'll take care of the relief. You worry about keeping Sutton and March occupied with thoughts of great riches." At his questioning look, she added, "Surely the promise of another chamber to explore will keep them from even thinking about me."

Josh left Teri in the tent and went in search of their evening meal. He'd about made good his escape with a basket of food, when Kevin March came up beside him.

"Where's your wife? We hoped you'd both join us for our evening meal."

"She's in the tent," Josh explained. "The tension of the afternoon has given her a beast of a headache. I thought I'd just grab a few things and take her some tea to calm her nerves."

"I take it she's not used to the dangers of a dig."

"No, this is the first time she's ever come with me. And likely the last."

Kevin chuckled, but sobered quickly. "I have to admit, I was scared speechless today. Thank you for being so levelheaded."

"I was just as anxious to save my own skin, as anyone else's." As an afterthought, Josh added, "I'd like to go down with you in the morning before we leave, to help assess the viability of the new site."

"I'd appreciate that," March admitted.

"Good night then," Josh said as he turned toward the tent he shared with Teri. "I'll see you at first light."

He entered the tent moments later. Teri sat crossed-legged on their bed, tearing one of the cotton shirts he'd claimed on their first night into long even strips. Carefully, she wrapped the relief in one of the strips. He stood there watching her work, mesmerized by the simple glow of her skin, the way the moonlight coming through the side of the tent cast shadows across her loose hair.

He felt the familiar itch of sensual greed, of wanting to comb his fingers through her hair, of wanting to touch and taste every inch of her body. At the moment, she seemed as perfect to him as the ancient piece of history she so carefully cradled in her grasp.

"So, you've figured out a way to keep our treasure safe, have you?" he asked.

"I think so. I'm going to wrap the other strips around my middle to create a pouch then tuck the wrapped piece in between the folds of the cloth. As long as I don't tuck my shirt into my jeans, I should be able to hide the additional thickness."

"If you need to, you could always wear the other cotton shirt over the top of your tee shirt like a loose jacket."

"I'm hoping it won't come to that. The extra layers are going to be warm enough as it is."

"We'd better call it a night," he said suddenly, dropping the dirty camp shorts and shirt to the ground. Stepping out of his boxers, he turned to her and added, "I told March I'd go down into the dig with him in the morning to make sure it's viable to work."

"I don't want you to go down there again," she admitted. "It's not safe."

He slipped into the bed and turned back the blanket in invitation. Teri quickly removed her clothes and slid in beside him. The moment their naked bodies touched, he became aroused. As tired and as sore as he was, he knew it would be useless to deny how badly he wanted her, or how eager he was to make love to her. Still, he felt he had to explain.

"I was the one who decided to break through the wall and show them the chamber. I can't in good conscience let something else happen because I didn't assure the safety of the dig."

"I admire you for that, I really do." She pressed her mouth to his for a quick kiss before telling him, "I also have reservations about something happening to you and my being left alone without even an iota of a clue as to how to get home."

"I promise you nothing is going to happen."

Teri splayed her hand across his chest and then ran her flattened palm down the length of his body until she could enclose his erection. "You mean tomorrow, right? Nothing's going to happen tomorrow."

With the first stroke of her hand, he drew in a long draft of air. "Yes, tomorrow." Josh eased her across his body until she sat atop his aching arousal. The moment she started to move, he conceded, "However, tonight is a totally different story."

Chapter 8

Teri packed up what little belongings they had and double-checked the security of the cotton pouch fastened around her middle. As an afterthought, she slipped her fingertips into the watch pocket of her jeans and felt the cool press of the pink stone. Everything was as it should be. Well, almost everything.

Josh, Kevin March, and Sutton had gone below ground to assess the dig and explore the chamber nearly two hours earlier. With each passing minute, her apprehension grew. What if something had happened? She couldn't bear the idea of being alone in this strange time and place, of being without Josh.

One of Sutton's graduate students arrived at the tent moments later, his light knock drawing her from her thoughts. "Mrs. Cain?"

"Yes."

"The professor and Dr. Cain have returned from the dig site. The supply truck will be leaving in twenty minutes."

"Thank you. Tell my husband I'll be there shortly."

"I will." The young man turned and left.

She spared one last glance around the tent, content she'd forgotten nothing and then stepped out into the hot midday sun.

Josh and Sutton were standing beside the truck, lost in conversation. She approached cautiously, careful to keep herself out of Sutton's direct line of sight.

"Thank you, Professor Cain," Sutton said, offering Josh an envelope.

"What's this?" Josh asked.

"An honorarium of sorts for finding the chamber."

"That's not necessary."

"It's not much, given we've not made any income off this site as yet, but it will tide you over until you can track down your belongings."

Josh took the envelope from Sutton's hand. "Thank you."

Sutton turned toward Teri. "Don't forget my offer. You do your best, Mrs. Cain, to coax your husband to return."

She shaded her eyes and met Sutton's gaze. "I'll do what I can, Professor. However, as Josh said, everything will depend on our getting back our belongings, especially our papers."

Josh helped her into the waiting truck and then took a seat at her side. The driver climbed behind the wheel and set the vehicle in motion. When they came to the end of the first long road the driver slowed to make the turn. That was when she saw it, the one structure she could identify without Josh's help.

The Sphinx, in all its magnificent glory.

As if he could sense her wonder, Josh grasped her hand and gave it a gentle squeeze. "If you like, we can come back and look at it properly after we're settled in at the hotel."

She shook her head. "No, I just want to get to Cairo, and eventually go home."

She sat back in her seat and weathered the sixteen hot, dusty miles to Cairo, optimistic that somewhere in the ancient city the next step in their adventure would begin.

The driver let them out in front of the Cairo Arms hotel, a surprisingly elegant establishment in the middle of the city. The moment they stepped into the lobby, she found herself overwhelmed with the opulence, the grandeur of the huge entryway. Decorated with fine antiques and thick Persian carpets, she wondered if the money Sutton gave them, combined with the sale of the relief, would be enough to cover their expenses.

Josh checked them into the hotel, using part of the honorarium to secure them a modest room overlooking the nearby market.

"I'll slip next door to one of the shops and bargain for a change of clothes," he said. "Why don't you take the key and go up to the room? I'm sure you'd love a hot bath."

She took the key from his hand. "Please don't be gone long. I won't be comfortable by myself."

"I shouldn't be more than a half hour," he assured her.

She opened the door to their room and then shut and locked it behind her. As Josh had suggested, she ran a bath and sank blissfully beneath the water, allowing the dust and dirt of the past few days to dissolve away along with the worst of the tension gripping her body.

The moment she stepped out of the tub, a knock sounded at the door. Wrapping herself in a bath towel, she went to the door to let Josh in.

She was about to turn the lock when the hairs on the back of her arms stood up; the nerves running along her spine tingled. She turned, certain there was someone standing behind her. Yet, there was nothing, no one, there.

The heavy knock sounded again and her pulse raced. Surely, if it were Josh, he would say something.

"Who is it?" she asked.

"Room service, Mrs. Cain," the man said, his accent thick but understandable. "Dr. Cain requested we deliver an afternoon meal promptly at three. It's is now three and five."

Teri looked down at the towel and realized she couldn't answer the door as she was. About to ask the man to come back in a few minutes, she was saved from doing so when she heard the welcome sound of Josh's voice.

"Teri, it's me," he said. "Unlock the door, please."

"Okay, just a minute." She slipped the lock and then scurried across the room and back into the bathroom just as Josh came through the door, pushing the serving cart and juggling a handful of brown paper and twine wrapped packages at the same time.

Once he'd closed the door behind him, she came back into the room.

He gave her a quick scan and wagged his expressive brows. "And here I thought you were being cautious toward a stranger. I had no idea you were half naked."

"I was waiting for you to return. I didn't want to put my dirty clothes back on after that wonderful bath."

He waved his hand toward the packages he'd tossed on the bed. "Why don't you have something to eat and go through the clothes to make sure they fit while I take a turn in the tub?"

"Aren't you hungry?" she asked.

"Not as hungry as I am dirty."

She took the lid off the serving plates and found an array of fruits, vegetables, and chilled meats. As hungry as she was, the idea of going through the clothing appealed to her even more than food. Replacing the covers on the plates, she unwrapped the parcels, dumping the contents in the middle of the bed.

In the pile, she found two changes of undergarments, both more functional than seductive, yet exactly the right size. Next she unearthed two pairs of lightweight slacks and two cotton, button-up shirts and a pair of sandals and, again, much to her amusement, a perfect fit.

"You're awfully good at this," she called out through the bathroom door.

"Good at what?" he asked.

"Judging ladies clothing sizes."

He laughed, the warm sound drawing her to the bathroom

door. When she stood on the threshold, he looked over at her and smiled.

"My skill at choosing clothing comes from studying the human anatomy, a necessity when trying to identify remains. Having had a rather thorough study of your anatomy over the past few days, it wasn't difficult to choose the correct size."

Heat crept into her cheeks. Yet, the thought of spending more time studying Josh's anatomy intrigued her and encouraged a boldness she'd not often felt.

"I don't suppose you'd care to do more research." She hooked a finger in the knot at the top of her towel and twisted, allowing the thick terry material to fall to the floor at her feet.

Josh sat up in the tub and, with a crook of his finger, beckoned her forward. "The nicest thing about these deep, claw-foot tubs is that they're big enough for two."

By the time they actually got around to eating, the food had lost a lot of its appeal, except for the dates. As she was quickly discovering, she loved dates. She also loved the soft cotton clothing Josh had chosen; the finely woven material caressed her skin like a lover's hands. Like Josh's hands.

While she replaced the empty plates on the serving cart and pushed it outside the room, Josh worked on organizing their few meager possessions, and putting together a safe hiding place for the relief. The pink stone, now safely tucked inside the pocket of his new khakis, would go with them wherever they went.

"I have a couple more errands to run this evening, one of which has to be completed before seven."

"I'm coming with you," she insisted.

Josh paused for a moment, as if he were considering whether or not to take her along. He finally nodded and turned toward the door. "Then, let's get going. We'll want to be back before dark."

Their first stop was to a local shop where Josh purchased a compact leather pouch and the few tools necessary to clean the encrusted relief. Moments later, they were on the move again.

"Where are we going now?" she asked.

"I want to drop by the museum. I'm interested in seeing exactly what they've identified so far, and what is still missing."

"You're looking specifically for the statue, aren't you?"

"Yes, the statue and any other significant pieces from Tuthmosis III's tomb. We already know, they've not yet labeled Hatshepsut's artifacts, nor even acknowledged her reign."

"What happens if we actually find the statue? Then what?"

"That's what has me most concerned. If we find the statue, we could always give the museum the stone and allow them to place it back in the ivory idol where it belongs. However, that doesn't guarantee the statue and stone will ever make it back to Hatshepsut. And, without reuniting the *Eye* with its owner, we may not be sent home."

"Speaking of home, what do you think is happening there? Do they realize we're gone? Are they looking for us?"

Josh shook his head. "I'm not sure. I haven't a clue how this all works."

"I'm certain, if they realize we're missing, they'll search for us."

"I worry about my girls," he admitted. "They've always known there was danger in my job. Every dig presents a certain amount of risk. However, to just disappear—"

She stopped short, grabbing Josh's arm to still his forward progress. When he turned to face her, she laid her hand against his cheek. "I know they have faith you'll return. Just as I have faith you'll figure this all out and get us home safely."

"*We'll* figure this out," he corrected. "Don't think for one moment you're not an important part of the solution."

Josh's words moved her more than any she'd ever heard. She'd pictured herself as an innocent bystander in all of this, a willing assistant to Josh's expertise. Yet, his simple statement had given her hope, desire, to be more than just a bystander, to be as Josh said part of the ultimate solution.

"How far to the museum?" she asked when Josh turned down a long, dusty street.

"Tahrir Square is just around the next corner."

Josh picked up a faster pace and she literally had to run to keep up with him. Once they'd turned the corner, her hurried footsteps stalled. There, in front of her, was the most magnificent structure she'd seen since they'd passed the Sphinx.

"It's massive," she said, "and the artistry around the building entrance is breathtaking."

"The building is fairly new, given the current year. It was completed in 1902, a few years later they began moving the displays from the previous location, a process that's still taking place."

"Where will we go first?" she asked.

"To the Royal Mummy room. If I'm not mistaken, there should be at least two dozen sets of remains. Hopefully, what we're looking for will be among them."

She followed Josh from display to display, each set of royal remains identified by a simple engraved plaque. The largest of the displays was only in the design stages but she could tell the area would be massive once complete.

"I wonder whose remains will be placed there," she said, pointing to the open space.

"In modern times, that's where they placed Tutankhamun. I assume it's the same now and they're preparing for Carter's discovery."

"And this one?" she asked, nodding toward the next display.

"Seti II, fifth ruler of the nineteenth dynasty."

They came across Hatshepsut's father's tomb, Tuthmosis I next, the very simple display at odds with some of the more lavish finds. She found herself drawn to the unusual carvings in the cramped area. It was a moment before she realized Josh had moved on to yet another set up.

"There," Josh said, pointing toward an exhibit in progress. "Tuthmosis III, or at least the beginnings of the display."

"No statue," Teri said, her voice filled with disappointment. "We're back to square one."

"Not necessarily. It's incomplete. There are likely many more pieces to add."

Turning away from the half-finished exhibit, Josh headed toward the front of the museum.

"Where are you going now?" she asked.

"I want to find the curator or his assistant. We need to know what items still need to be placed on display."

As she had on their walk over, she picked up her pace until she was right behind Josh. "How will you broach the subject without giving too much away?"

"I'm not sure yet, but I'll think of something."

Teri had no doubt he would. If there was one thing, among many, Josh excelled at it was thinking on his feet.

Chapter 9

They waited patiently while the museum host went in search of the curator, Dr. Goodson.

"If memory serves," Josh began, "Dr. Goodson was instrumental in getting the museum up and running in less than two years after he took over. His approach to the selection and organization of artifacts has been copied around the world many times over the past fifty to sixty years."

"Hopefully, he'll be opened minded to our search."

"Yes, hopefully."

The sound of footsteps drew her attention. A very distinguished-looking man with salt and pepper hair and a finely trimmed handlebar mustache approached.

"Good afternoon," the man said. "I understand you wish to speak with me."

Josh held out his hand. "I'm Professor Joshua Cain, Princeton University. This is my wife, Teri. You must be Dr. Charles Goodson."

"Yes, temporary curator of the museum," the man acknowledged. "How may I be of assistance, Professor?"

"We were wondering if there were any other pieces not yet displayed in the Tuthmosis III exhibit. I'd heard mention of the possible existence of an ivory statue and was wondering if it had been recovered during excavation."

"Not to my knowledge. However, there are a few boxes left to be unpacked."

"Is there an inventory available?" Josh asked.

She could sense the moment Goodson's demeanor

changed, the moment he realized Josh's questions weren't just random curiosity.

"Just what is your interest in this supposed statue, Dr. Cain?"

"To tell the truth, it pertains to some research I uncovered recently. Reports of an Egyptian curse set in place centuries ago."

Teri watched the play of expressions across both Josh's and Charles Goodson's face, each man sizing up the other in terms of trust.

"A curse?" Goodson repeated. "Surely a man of science such as yourself doesn't give a fig about a supposed curse."

"My point exactly, which is why I want to dispel the notion right from the start, beginning with a statue which most likely doesn't exist."

"We can check the inventory if you'd like," Goodson offered, motioning for them to follow him to his office. "Although it's unlikely any such statue will appear on the list, even if it does exist. Ivory, especially good-grade ivory, tends to be a favorite of grave robbers. And, as we've found out over the past few years, a number of the recently excavated tombs were victims of these dastardly thieves."

"If we can eliminate its existence from the excavation, I will at least have a starting place for my paper." Josh told the man.

They followed Goodson into the cramped, box-littered office and waited while he pushed one pile of papers aside only to uncover another in the same disarray.

"It's here somewhere," Goodson said. "I just have to find it. I can't tell you how disorganized this move has been. They kept very shoddy records at the last location. I'm hoping, during my short tenure, to re-organize everything."

A thought, however incomplete, came to her in a flash. "You know, Dr. Goodson, my husband and I will be here in Cairo for another few days. We would be happy to lend a hand in any way we can. I do have cataloging experience and my husband is an expert in the field of identification and dating."

She turned toward Josh, her quick thinking drawing his smile.

"I could use a volunteer or two," Goodson admitted. "Of course, you realize you would not be given access to any of the restricted areas."

"Yes, of course," she agreed. "We wouldn't expect unlimited access. However, I'm sure there are some minor artifacts, some non-essential items which require entering into inventory."

The curator sighed deeply. "Thousands unfortunately and I'm only one man. Unless of course you count the two pre-grad students who are more interested in discovering each other than any ancient treasure."

"I can guarantee you, my wife and I would be dedicated to the work at hand," Josh promised.

Goodson lifted a folder from the bottom of the pile of paperwork. "Here it is, the complete inventory from Tuthmosis III's tomb."

He handed Josh the file. Josh thumbed through it quickly, his narrowed gaze scanning the three pages once, twice, and finally a third time. She could tell by his stoic expression, he'd not found a listing for the statue, or even mention of its existence.

"You were correct, Dr. Goodson, no record of an ivory statue." Handing the folder back, Josh added, "Thank you for allowing me to check."

"If your offer of assistance still stands," Goodson said, "I can arrange for temporary papers for you and your lovely wife."

"Yes, we'd like to help," Teri told him. "We could come back tomorrow morning if you can make the arrangements."

Goodson's mustache wiggled when he smiled. "Between

ten and eleven would be smashing."

"We'll be here," Josh confirmed.

"What's our next step?" she asked once they'd left the museum and stopped at a nearby café.

"I'm hoping to find a buyer for the piece I brought from the dig. I can't sell it through the usual channels, but I'm sure a word dropped here and there will scrounge up some willing customers."

"It sounds so dark and nefarious."

Josh chuckled. "I suppose it does seem so, doesn't it." He took a sip of his coffee. "I'll go and spread the word among a few shopkeepers, then meet you back at the hotel in an hour."

"Can't I come with you?"

He shook his head. "It's too dangerous."

"But—" she began, only to have him interrupt.

"I don't mean dangerous as in life-threatening. It would be unlikely we'd get a buyer with a crowd around. All communication must be kept to a bare minimum. Let's face it, what self-respecting artifact pusher would take his wife with him on a potential offering?"

She forced a chuckle, nodded her understanding, and did her best to hide her frown of concern. She felt as if every nerve ending in her body were on edge and not in a good way. She closed her eyes briefly and drew in a breath. As it had before, when Josh went back down into Sutton's dig, the very thought of being left alone to fend for herself in such a strange place and time set the rhythm of her pulse on a frantic pace.

The walk back to the hotel took them past a number of shops, most of which displayed some form of relic in their window. None, she noted, were of museum quality, but each piece held its own mystery, its own place in the grand scheme of Egyptian history.

They arrived at the hotel less than a half hour later and

Josh escorted her to their room. "Lock the door behind me," he told her.

"Are you sure I can't come with you? I could wait somewhere nearby."

"All alone?" he asked. When she shook her head, rejecting the thought, he said, "I'll not send anyone to the room for anything, so don't open the door no matter what. "

"Don't worry," she agreed willingly, "I won't."

The moment she shut the door, Teri slid the safety latch into place. Despite the fact she knew she was alone in the room, she couldn't help but check beneath every chair, the entire bathroom, and in every closet.

She moved from door to window and back again, double-checking the latch for a third time until, finally, she stood at the window and nudged the curtain aside with the tips of her fingers until she could see out to the main street. In the courtyard below a group of men sat drinking wine and playing board games on rickety folding tables, their laughter interspersed with comments in a language she didn't understand.

Sliding the curtain back into place, Teri crossed the room, finally taking a seat at the foot of the bed. The room was stuffy, yet she dared not open the window until Josh returned. Once she'd settled herself on the bed, she lay back against the pillow and attempted to count the dots in the patterned ceiling. Within moments she began drifting in and out of sleep.

A cool breeze brushed across her skin, pulling her back toward wakefulness. She smoothed her hand across her forearm and felt tiny goose bumps beneath her fingertips. She turned her head from side to side and opened her eyes. The sight greeting her sent her heart rate into overdrive.

"Who are you?" the woman asked.

Teri pressed her eyes shut tight in an effort to dispel the vision, to wake up from what was obviously a dream. When she opened her eyes again, she could make out the faint image of a woman standing at the foot of her bed.

She should have been frightened, paralyzed with fear in fact. Every fiber in her being screamed panic! Yet, for some inexplicable reason she wasn't. Instead, she found herself struck by the woman's classic beauty. Her jet-black hair hung in a straight frame around her face, falling just short of her waist. Her huge dark eyes were rimmed with black eyeliner. The flowing robe she wore was a plush cloth of deepest purple, trimmed in gold thread. The expensive garment hugged her ample curves.

"I'm Teri, Teri Hunter."

"From where do you hail, Teri Hunter?"

"Excuse me?" The woman's speech seemed stilted, as if she struggled with the English language. Rather than answer her question, Teri asked, "Who are you?"

"I am Anukahaten, guardian of the queen-Pharaoh's tomb."

"You're the guardian of Hatshepsut's tomb?" Teri asked. The urge to pinch herself awake was overwhelming, but not as tempting as the thought of asking a few more questions before she did.

"Yes. It is so. Many years ago, I failed my queen and now I struggle to make things right."

"I know about the stone," she admitted, "and the curse. Can you tell us where to find the statue?"

"I only know it is here, close to Cairo, but I know not where."

"Can you at least tell me what it looks like, so we'll know when we've found it?"

"It is barely as tall as the length of a man's hand," Anukahaten began, "no bigger than a . . ."

Anukahaten's vision began to fade, her voice trailing off, interrupted by an insistent tapping, an intrusion Teri wanted desperately to ignore.

"Teri, are you in there?" Josh asked, the sound of his raised voice drawing Teri fully awake.

"Sorry," she called out. "I'll be right there."

She slid from the bed and crossed the room on shaky legs, her mind tripping over itself in an effort to remember the details of her dream. When she lifted the security latch from the door and opened it, Josh stepped inside.

"I was starting to worry," he told her. "I'd knocked quite a few times."

"I was asleep," she told him, "and having the weirdest dream."

"That's not surprising, given all we've been through in the past few days. Dreams, even nightmares, would be normal."

"Are you familiar with the name Anukahaten?" she asked.

"It sounds familiar, although I'm not sure from where."

"In my dream this woman said her name was Anukahaten and she was the guardian of Hatshepsut's tomb. She asked who I was and where I was from."

"A dream?" he repeated in question. "Are you sure you were asleep?"

"Well of course I was asleep. How else could I have imagined her?"

Instead of responding, Josh took her by the hand and led her to the overstuffed settee. When they were seated, he explained, "It's not uncommon in Egyptian folklore for people to have visions, not dreams but wide-awake visions of people from ancient times. Especially when there is a supposed curse involved with the dynasty or noble they are exploring."

"A vision? You think I had a vision?"

"It wouldn't be the first on record, especially if we're getting close. It's said the guardian of the curse, in this case the guardian of Hatshepsut's tomb, might come to aid in the discovery."

"I see we've stepped back into the realm of creepy again," she teased, the lighthearted comment more for her own sanity than levity.

"Did she say where we could find the statue? Did you ask?"

"Well, of course I asked. However, someone tapping on my door scared my so-called vision away before she could tell me."

"Damn. This vision, Anukahaten, could possibly have been our best lead."

Really? Was he totally insane? Preferring the reality of a proposed buyer for their artifact rather than the possibility of a vision, she asked, "How did your search for a buyer go?"

"I expect we'll have at least two or three interested parties by morning. Bids will be left at the front desk in sealed envelopes. I'll respond to the best offer."

"May I go with you this time?" she asked.

He shrugged. "It will all depend on who wins the bid and where I'm to meet them." He paused then added, "It might be better for you to stay here in case Anukahaten comes back."

"I'm supposed to wait here for a vision?"

He grinned at her, his smile easing some of the tension from her body. "It would be the quickest way to end our search."

"Once we're home again, remind me never to accept a job involving non-fiction authors of Egyptian history or mummies. From now on, I only intend to represent fiction writers. At least their stories are made up and won't land me in the middle of an ancient curse."

"Deal, as long as you remind me to never write another mass market book. From now on, it's textbooks only." Josh raised himself from the settee and offered her his hand. "It's getting late. If we're going to be at the museum by ten, we'd better get to bed."

"Yes, I suppose we should."

Teri used the bathroom first, taking time to brush her teeth, draw a comb through her hair, and don the thin cotton gown Josh had purchased for her at the market. Not that she expected to wear it for long. She spared a quick thought for their lovemaking earlier in the day, the lure of the deep tub urging them into a somewhat frenetic romp between the sheets.

Josh was definitely an accomplished lover and being with him was exhilarating. And, for the first time in her life, the lovemaking was also calming. There was no need for game play or dancing around the *will she or won't she* scenario. No wondering whether or not the night would end satisfactorily for both parties. They were just two adults enjoying one another, no strings attached.

Lovemaking with Josh was perfect.

"About time," Josh teased when she returned. "I thought maybe you were having another vision."

"I didn't have a vision," she insisted. "It was just a dream."

Josh leaned closer and pressed a chaste kiss to her forehead. "If you say so."

Before she could respond, he closed the bathroom door between them.

She turned back the covers on the big bed, certain they'd not need anything more than a sheet on such a hot and humid night. Josh had opened the window earlier, but it had done nothing to cool off the room. What she wouldn't give at that moment, she realized, for her condo's central air conditioning.

Josh came out of the bathroom moments later wearing little more than his smile. Much to her embarrassment, she couldn't help but stare. Even in a flaccid state, his body was impressive. When he climbed into the bed and drew her close, she willingly rolled over and sequestered herself in his embrace.

He pressed his lips to her temple. "I wonder what Mrs. DeChambeau is thinking, given we've disappeared with her husband's treasure in hand?"

As he spoke, Josh fingered the buttons at the bodice of her gown, casually sliding the first three from their holes.

"I'm sure she's not worried," Teri said, her breath catching when Josh pushed the gown to the side and enclosed her breast in his warm hand.

"Until we're sent back, we have no way of knowing how this little adventure has affected current time."

The words had barely left his lips when he bent his head and took her mouth in a slow, deep kiss. In between kisses, he tugged at the arms of the gown until he'd drawn them down around her wrists.

"I'm not sure why I bothered to even put this gown on," she admitted, her frustration mounting when she realized her arms were captive in the soft cloth and preventing her from reaching for Josh, from stroking his chest and teasing him in the same manner in which he would soon tease her.

Josh chuckled as he slid the first sleeve across her wrist, setting her arm free. "I'm not sure why I bought it. I've no intention of letting you wear it, at least not for long."

The moment the unwanted gown was thrown aside, Josh rolled onto his back and drew Teri across his body. The coarse hairs on his chest tickled her breasts, drawing her nipples into tight, wanton buds. The feel of his arousal pressing against her thigh urged her to part her legs, to find a more fitting spot for his length.

"Teri," he whispered against her ear, "just the feel of your body atop mine drives me insane. I've never, ever become so aroused with so little effort. I'd thought, after the first time we made love, the ache, the immediate desire would stop, but it hasn't. If anything, it's increased."

"I know. It's the same for me." She raised herself up on her hands and leaned forward, thrusting her breast toward his mouth. When he closed his lips around the turgid crest she cried out his name. She lowered herself over his erection, her body damp with need and ready to welcome him inside. "See," she said when he was fully sheathed, "no need for lengthy preliminaries. No more than your touch, or a few kisses, and I'm ready, willing, and anxious."

Josh rocked his hips, stroking them both in the process. She snuggled closer until she lay stretched out across his frame. In contrast to the more physical lovemaking earlier in the day, this joining was slow, measured, and infinitely enjoyable.

They took turns, Josh raising and lowering his hips, Teri reciprocating with a shift of her own. They kissed, they fondled, yet never attempted to pick up the pace. She couldn't remember ever being this aroused, this totally consumed. She climaxed once, twice, the clenching of her muscles each time she came drawing Josh's repeated groans.

She pressed her lips to Josh's, stroking his lower lip with her tongue until he opened his mouth and accepted her deepened kiss. She raised her bottom, and then lowered herself again, stroking him slowly, completely.

"You're driving me crazy," he said, his voice little more than a growl between kisses.

She repeated the lifting and lowering a second and third time, each long stroke of her body matched by the equally deep thrust of her tongue.

"You can put a stop to the insanity," she whispered. "If you want to."

He shook his head, clearly not ready to end the languid seduction any sooner than necessary. "More," he said, "I want more, and then some."

His heartfelt plea drew yet another strong climax from her body causing her to grasp at the sheets beneath them and hang on for dear life until the latest wave of excitement coursed through her body. Her flushed skin tingled from head to toe, everywhere Josh touched she burned. She closed her eyes and waited for the last tremble to recede.

"Who is this man you are coupling with?"

She heard the voice, Anukahaten's voice, but when she opened her eyes there was no one there other than Josh.

"Did you hear that?" she asked.

"If you're talking about the pounding of my heart, yes I heard it, still hear it." Josh took her hand and pressed it to his chest. "Feel that? It's what you do to me." He wrapped his arms around her back and rolled over in the bed until he hovered above her. "Yet, still I want more. I want to drive into you so deeply, so completely, it will seem like we've swallowed each other whole."

Digging her fingertips into his sculpted buttocks, she urged him forward. "I'd like that too. Very much."

Chapter 10

Teri rolled onto her side and laid her hand on Josh's chest, idly running her fingertips through the hairs running from breastbone to belly. She loved the feel of his muscles bunching and jumping just beneath the surface of his skin when she flattened her hand and ran her palm across his middle.

"I heard the voice again." She stilled the slow stroke of her hand and waited for his response.

"When?"

"Earlier, when we were making love. She asked who you were." She lowered her hand, enclosing his semi-erection in her grasp. "Her exact words were, 'Who is this man you are coupling with?'"

"She was watching us?"

Josh's entire body tensed and he circled her wrist and squeezed gently, effectively stopping the progress she'd made at arousing him yet again.

"Does that bother you?" she asked.

"It doesn't bother you?"

"She's a figment of my imagination, Josh. A by-product of our strange situation and nothing more."

"So, you do believe we've traveled through time and place."

She shifted at his side, turning until she could look around the room. "I have no choice in the matter. We're here, nearly a hundred years and thousands of miles from where we began."

"How can you accept one strange occurrence and not the other? If someone, or something, can bring us years and miles from home, why can't there be visions from centuries past?"

He had a point, not one she cared to concede, but a point all the same.

"I believe the time travel is what caused the dream, or vision if you will, not the other way around."

"Perhaps we need to look at this more logically, as in why would you dream of someone you had no idea even existed until she came to you in a vision. If she hadn't actually spoken to you, could you have pulled the name Anukahaten out of a hat?"

Another good point she wasn't quite ready to accept.

"Rather than being logical this late at night, perhaps what we need a good night's sleep to put this all in perspective," she suggested, rolling over and facing away from the temptation of Josh's body.

"Sleep, per chance to dream, my lady," he teased.

She released a long sigh. "Thanks, Josh. Now I'll never nod off."

The alarm on Josh's watch sounded promptly at eight-thirty, waking her from a sound sleep. From an uneventful sleep. She rolled over, intent on reaching for Josh only to find his side of the bed empty, and the beeping watch lying on the pillow next to her. Still half asleep, she grabbed the offending object and pressed the button on the casing.

She sat up in the bed and pushed the hair from her eyes until she could scan the room from door, to window, to far wall. The door to the bathroom was open, the room empty. She'd barely had time to wonder where Josh had gone, when the sound of a key turning in the lock of the door had her pulling the sheet up to her chin in an effort to cover her naked breasts.

A moment later, Josh stepped into the room. "Oh, good, you're awake," he said. "I've brought breakfast."

"Where were you?" she asked.

"I couldn't sleep so I thought I go downstairs and see if we had any takers for our artifact."

"And?" she prompted.

"As I expected, there were two bids. However, one is significantly higher than the other, so that's where we'll go."

"We? I can come as well?" The idea of tagging along on Josh's illicit sale set her pulse rate thrumming.

"I see no reason why not. The buyer's home is in a rather well-to-do part of town."

"What about the other bidder? Do you have any idea why the offers were so far apart?"

"From what I could tell by the note the second man left, he must be a collector of odds and ends. Or, more precisely, the leftovers no other collector wants."

"When do we go?" she asked.

"As soon as you're dressed and we've had our breakfast," he said. "The stop is on our way to the museum. So, barring any complications with the sale, we should still be able to make our ten-thirtyish commitment to Dr. Goodson."

She pushed the sheet aside and literally jumped from the bed in her haste to get on with their day. Josh's wolf-whistle barely registered as she scampered for the bathroom, dragging her cotton slacks, gauzy shirt, and undergarments with her.

"You know, we could send word to the museum indicating we'll be a bit late," he suggested, his tone a mixture of teasing and lurid suggestion.

"I thought you were self-conscious about being watched by some other-world spirit, Dr. Cain?"

"Not *that* self-conscious."

Teri came back through the bathroom door, pulling her hair into a ponytail atop her head as she went. "Too late, I'm dressed, and famished." Peering into the brown sack on the table, she asked, "What'd you bring to eat?"

They caught a ride to the address on the piece of paper containing the highest bid. The local merchant stopped his truck at the end of a long driveway leading up to an old, but well-kept home and let them out.

"Thank you," Josh said in Egyptian Arabic, passing the elderly man a couple of coins for his trouble.

"What other languages do you speak?" Teri asked as they negotiated the uneven walkway toward the front of the house.

"French, Spanish, and another two dialects of Arabic. My German is too rusty to claim. What about you?"

"A bit of Italian, a gift from my great-grandmother on my mother's side and good old English." The thought of Josh seducing her with phrases murmured in French sent a shiver up her back.

They climbed the limestone stairs to the front door of the home and Josh lifted the heavy brass knocker and let it fall into place. Within moments a frail man, his back hunched over from age and most likely a life of hard work, answered the door.

"May I help you?" He spoke English, much to her relief.

"We're here to see D. P. about an acquisition," Josh explained, showing the man the note as proof of their invitation.

The man stepped back, allowing them to enter the cluttered entranceway. Everywhere Teri looked, she saw bits and pieces of history. Every table, every wall, even the sides of the wide oak staircase held some artifact, some piece of limestone or gilded metal. Teri wondered if they might find the ivory statue among the mysterious D. P.'s collection.

They were escorted to the library just off the main entrance and offered seats around an oval table its top made of inlaid marble. Josh ran his hand across the surface, examining the piece with an art historian's eye. Beneath the sleeve of her blouse, she could feel the hairs rise on her arms, a tingle invade every nerve ending, the heightening of her senses driven by the memory of Josh's touch.

A servant entered with a tray of coffee and breads and sat everything in the center of the beautiful table.

"Mr. Parsket will be with you shortly," the woman said, her accent thick but her English easily understandable.

Josh lifted the coffee pot and poured himself a cup. "Would you like some?" he asked, turning in Teri's direction.

She shook her head. "One cup per day is my limit. The coffee here is much stronger than I'm used to. I'll be bouncing off the walls if I drink another."

Josh leaned closer to her side and whispered, "If this Mr. Parsket is who I think he is, we've come across one of the most accomplished collectors of the early twentieth century."

Again, she wondered about the elusive ivory statue. "Could he possibly have the statue?"

"I'm not sure, but I intend to ask," Josh confirmed.

"Intend to ask what?" The question drew their attention to the opposite side of the room.

A tall, elegant woman stood framed in the doorway, her gray hair piled high atop her head, her clothes obviously tailor-made for her slim frame.

Josh stood, drawing Teri to her feet as well. When the woman reached their side, he held out his hand. "I'm Professor Joshua Cain, Princeton University. This is my wife, Teri."

The woman clasped Josh's hand in hers. "I am Ariel Parsket. My husband will be joining us momentarily." Motioning toward the chairs, she said, "Please, sit back down." She took the seat opposite Teri and added, "I understand you've brought something for our collection."

"Yes." Josh withdrew the relief from his shirt pocket. Carefully unwrapping the limestone piece, he laid the linen cloth down on the table first, and placed the artifact on top. "I've brought a seventeenth dynasty relief from the tomb of the high priest said to have watched over and given spiritual guidance to Tetisheri, consort of the Pharaoh Sekenenre Tao I."

"Sekenenre Tao I," Ariel Parsket repeated. "One of the most violent times in Egyptian history if I'm not mistaken."

"Yes, war plagued the majority of his reign," Josh confirmed. "There are very few artifacts from Sekenenre Tao I's reign because of the battles and thievery."

"And you are certain this piece is authentic?" the woman asked.

"I am positive. I was in the tomb myself and viewed the wall engravings."

The library door opened and an elderly man entered. His gait extremely short, he walked with a cane and the assistance of a servant.

"I'm Donald Parsket," he said without preamble. "Let me see the piece you've brought."

Josh stood and lifted the relief into his hand. Donald Parsket had taken a seat at the nearby desk and Josh crossed the room to meet him there. Teri stood as well, and followed Josh to where the older man waited.

"I'm Dr. Joshua Cain. As I was telling your wife, I've discovered a limestone relief from the tomb of Pharaoh Sekenenre Tao I's consort, Tetisheri." As he spoke, Josh laid the relief down on the velvet covered jewelers pad in front of Parsket. "The writing here along the edges speak of the relationship between Sekenenre Tao I and Tetisheri, in quite vivid detail."

Teri leaned forward and stared at the cryptic edging, regretting the fact she'd never asked Josh for a translation. Her interest piqued, she made herself a mental note to ask him later when they'd returned to the hotel.

"This piece came from a registered dig?" Parsket asked.

Josh raised his head and met the man's gaze. "Not necessarily," he admitted. "Let's just say, it was a reward for saving the life of a fellow archaeologist."

"A reward given freely?" the man asked.

"Again, not necessarily."

Teri held her breath in anticipation of Parsket's response, thoroughly surprised and relieved when he laughed heartily.

"My concern is one of ownership, you understand," he said.

"The other members of the dig have no knowledge of the find," Josh explained. "They were more than satisfied with the additional items found due to my expertise. I felt it unnecessary to tell them about the relief."

Donald Parsket's laughter rang out a second time. "A man of opportunity, I like that. Tell me, Dr. Cain, are there any additional items you'd be willing to part with?"

"At this time, no. However, you can never tell what the future holds."

Ariel Parsket came to join them at the desk. "I believe you had a question for my husband, Dr. Cain."

"Yes, I do." Josh spared Teri a glance before explaining. "I'm working on a research project revolving around a supposed curse placed on the tomb of Tuthmosis III. I'm looking for an ivory statue said to have been taken from the tomb. It was intended to cradle a rare gem but the stone was allegedly stolen during the reign of Akhenaten as a gift for Nefertiti."

"We were wondering," Teri added, "if you either possess the statue as part of your collection or if you know who might have it."

"I know nothing of a curse, or a statue of such description," Parsket said. "However, I do have connections among avid collectors. I can put out some inquiries if you'd like."

"We'd appreciate it," Josh confirmed. "If you uncover anything word can be left at our hotel."

Donald Parsket opened his desk drawer, removed a metal strong box, and laid it on the desktop. "Let's get down to business, Dr. Cain." He opened the box to reveal a stack of mixed currency. "I believe the offer was for the bargain price of twenty thousand American dollars."

Josh nodded. "Yes, I believe it was."

Their business concluded, they said their goodbyes, eager to get another look at the museum's inventory. Parsket's driver dropped them off shortly before ten-thirty. Josh thanked the man and then helped Teri from the car before taking her hand and leading her up the steps of the museum.

"Well, we're solvent. The money will last quite a while and should provide us with enough cash to purchase the statue outright, assuming we can find it."

"With any luck," she agreed. "I'm more than ready to go home." She paused, then asked, "Mr. Parsket referred to the sale as a 'bargain price'. Was he being facetious?"

"No, not in the least. Had this been a legitimate sale rather than under-the-table, the price would have been considerably higher."

Dr. Goodson met them in the main entranceway, two paper identification tags waiting in his outstretched hand. "I've gained permission from the oversight committee to allow you access to the storage area in the basement, as well as the main areas of the museum. The only area restricted is the set up room and inside access to the Royal Mummy room."

"I'm sure there's plenty of work for us in the accessible areas," she said. "Just point us where you want us and we'll get to work."

Over the course of the next few hours, they'd discovered at least four ivory statues among the boxes. Unfortunately, none of them appeared to be the one they sought.

"What's this?" she asked, holding up a rather strange-looking object, eight inches in length, its ends were smoothly rounded and curved slightly, with a slight ridge halfway between each end.

Josh took the wooden carving from her hand and turned it over in his palm. "Do you really want to know?" he asked, his question followed by a muffled laugh.

"Of course," she said. "I find all these items interesting."

"It's a phallus, a sexual tool used to prepare a woman for the Pharaoh's plunder."

She felt a shiver crawl up her spine, her gaze assessing the item in question. "Prepare, in what way?"

"Not every Pharaoh was heterosexual, yet the need to carry on the bloodline was imperative. Often, the Pharaoh would engage in intercourse strictly with the goal of impregnating his wife. It was widely, and incorrectly, believed that the woman needed to achieve orgasm either prior to or during the sexual act in order for her womb to relax and accept the Pharaoh's seed. A servant or one of the Pharaoh's priests was often chosen to facilitate her readiness."

"So, despite the Pharaoh's sexual preference, he was able to perform with a woman?" Teri asked, her curiosity piqued by the idea of the strange ritual.

"For as little time as it took. According to many scholars who've spent countless hours studying the sexual and reproductive habits of the Pharaohs, it's been shown that while the servant or priest was providing the woman with gratification, the Pharaoh's male lover would provide pre-coital stimulation as well, often side-by-side with the wife's preparation."

"An orgy?"

"Not quite, but close. Once the woman had achieved orgasm at least once or twice, the Pharaoh was brought to the edge of his endurance. At that point, it was only a matter of penetration and a couple thrusts of the royal hips and it was over."

"Oh," she said simply, her response drawing another chuckle from Josh.

Teri picked up the next item, a long forged iron bar with a hook on the end. Offering the item up for Josh's inspection, she said, "I'm almost afraid to ask what this is."

Josh took the strange tool from her grasp and set it aside. "Let's just say, there was no pleasure involved with this. Rather, it was a means to an end after death."

They moved on to yet another unsealed box, removing item after item and spreading them out for Josh's identification.

The items ranged anywhere from household tools, to farming implements, to a number of other devices for sexual pleasure, for both the woman and the man. She decided Josh hadn't been joking when he'd said he'd left out as many of the sordid details of sexual practices as he'd put into his book.

By five o'clock, they'd unpacked, cataloged, and set up nearly two hundred minor pieces of Egyptian history. Taking turns, they'd written out descriptions on temporary placards to be placed next to the items scheduled for exhibit. The remaining items were labeled and placed on shelves in the underground storage area.

She turned full circle in the middle of the room and admired the extent of their efforts. "I don't know about you, but I'm tired and parched," she admitted. "I could use a cold beer right about now."

Josh shook his head and then said, "I'm not so sure you'd appreciate the beer they serve in 1922 Egypt. It's warm and with lots of foam. However, I would be willing to treat you to dinner and a glass or two of wine."

"You're quite the smooth talker, Dr. Cain. Not that I'm easy, but you had me at the mention of food."

They stopped at a local café not far from the hotel for an early-evening meal. She was pleasantly surprised by the extent of the rather non-descript establishment's menu and ordered herself a helping of chicken stew and bread. For dessert, she succumbed to the temptation of a rich honey-laden pastry.

"You were hungry," Josh said. "It must have been all our nefarious dealings and hard work that's made you so ravenous."

"That and the fact the food was not dried, chilled or otherwise preserved."

Josh took a sip of his coffee and bite from the corner of Teri's dessert. Playfully, she swatted at his hand and then relented, pushing the plate in his direction, offering him a second taste.

"You go on up to the room," Josh said when they entered the hotel lobby at half-past seven. "I'm going to check for messages and ask for a secure spot in the hotel's safe. I'm not comfortable carrying this money around."

"Try to hurry. I don't like opening the windows until you're there and I definitely want to take advantage of the evening breeze."

"I shouldn't be more than fifteen minutes, assuming they even have safe deposit boxes."

She unlocked the door to their room and stepped inside. The slowly setting sun cast an eerie glow over the walls and tiled floor. After securing the deadbolt, she turned toward the bathroom, intent on washing away the remnants of a hard day's work. She ran water into the sink and then leaned forward to dip her hands beneath the cool liquid, drawing a handful to her face.

"You are still looking for my queen's statue?"

Teri froze in place as the hairs on the back of her neck stood at attention. She raised her head and came face-to-face with the image of Anukahaten in the mirror above the sink.

"You're here," Teri said. "I'm awake, and you're here." She turned around to face the vision, yet found nothing but a solid wall behind her. Turning back, she blinked once, twice, at Anukahaten's reflection looking out at her from the beveled glass.

"I wish to ask if you have found the resting place for the *Eye of the Pharaoh*."

Teri swallowed back the lump in her throat and shook her head. "Not yet. We made contact with someone who may be able to help us, but we must wait for information."

"You will stay until you have found the statue?" Anukahaten asked.

"I didn't realize we had a choice," Teri admitted. "I thought we were stuck here until we'd completed our task."

"I could allow you to go home, if you so wish. I had hoped you and your consort would be the ones to find the statue."

"My consort?" Teri repeated. "It is Professor Cain who has the ability to find the statue, not me. He's the expert here. I'm only along by accident."

"He was brought here because the stone was in his possession. You were beckoned because of your personal history with Egypt. Only you can return the stone and the ivory idol to Queen Hatshepsut and end the curse."

"Me? I have no history with Egypt. I'm a born in the USA kind of girl."

Anukahaten shook her head; her glossy black hair swept across her bare dark-skinned shoulders. "I had once believed the curse could be broken by anyone, but I was wrong. I failed my queen. Now that I have seen you, I know it must be *you*." Anukahaten's vision began fading, as if she were backing down a long corridor.

"Can I ask you something before you go?"

"What is it you wish to know?"

"Do you watch over me, us, all the time?"

"No. You will know when I am here. You will be able to sense my presence."

Teri felt compelled to ask, "Could you stay away at night?"

"You wish to be alone with your lover," Anukahaten stated simply.

"Yes, please."

"I will only return at night if something of importance arises, Neferure."

"Who is Neferure?"

Rather than answer Teri's question, Anukahaten said, "Remember to ask your lover to translate the etchings on the relief from the priest's tomb."

"How did you know?" Teri asked.

When no answer came, she realized Anukahaten had gone. Teri braced herself against the marble sink and drew in a deep breath to calm the rapid beat of her heart. She couldn't stop the involuntary shudders running through her body when she thought back over this latest encounter. Not only were they being watched but, apparently, Anukahaten could also read her innermost thoughts.

Surely Anukahaten was wrong about her being the one to reunite the statue and stone. She couldn't fathom why she, of all people, would have been chosen. Anukahaten's visit raised far more questions than it answered.

For instance who, or what, was Neferure?

Chapter 11

Teri paced the width of their hotel room and back again, an unsettling feeling in the pit of her stomach making her even more nervous than usual. Relief swept through her when she heard Josh's familiar knock. Once she opened the door, Josh crossed the threshold in a rush and closed the door behind him just as quickly.

"Is something wrong?"

"No. However, it never hurts to be cautious, especially with so many people roaming around the lobby."

As he did both nights since they'd checked in, Josh opened the windows and glanced out over the courtyard before pinning back the lightweight curtains to make way for the evening breeze.

When he'd completed his evening ritual and taken a seat on the antique settee along the wall, Teri sat down beside him.

"I had another vision."

Josh sat forward, his big body drawn to full alert. "Anukahaten was here again?"

"Yes, and this time I was definitely awake."

"What did she say?"

"The most ridiculous thing you can imagine. According to Anukahaten, I'm the one who must find the statue and break the curse." The look of surprise on Josh's face was comical, drawing her smile.

"You?" he said.

Had she not known him better, she would have found his simple response condescending rather than one of complete shock.

"Yes, me. I told her she was wrong, you were the expert. She believes you're only here as my consort."

Josh relaxed a bit, a chuckle escaping his lips. "Well, it's nice to know I'm of some use."

"And, she promised to stay away at night. No more peeping vision."

"You actually asked her to stay away?"

"Certainly. As exciting as all this other-world contact is, making love with you is even better."

"What can I say? I'm the consort of choice."

She laughed then, her concern over Josh's reaction to Anukahaten's claim melting away as quickly as it came.

"Who is Neferure?"

"Hatshepsut's daughter," he explained. "Why do you ask?"

"Anukahaten mentioned it. As a matter of fact, I could have sworn she called me Neferure." Shaking her head, she added, "I must have heard her wrong."

Josh gathered her right hand in his and turned it over until her palm faced up. Gently, he ran his fingertip across the lifeline running from the base of her palm to the space between her thumb and forefinger.

"You have a very deep lifeline," he told her. "According to experts, the deeper the lifeline the more previous lives you've had."

"Previous lives? As in reincarnation?"

"Yes."

She felt an immediate tingling in her limbs, the hair on her arms electrified. Anukahaten was back. Watching her. Watching them.

"Do you believe in reincarnation, Josh?"

"Would it surprise you if I said yes?"

Teri placed Josh's hand against the rapidly beating pulse at the base of her throat. "She's back."

Josh flattened his palm against her neck and stroked the pulse point with his thumb, as if willing the racing to slow. "Any idea what she wants?"

"I think she was eavesdropping on our conversation." More pointedly, she added, "Even though she promised to stay away." Teri turned her head from side to side, doing her best to pick up on Anukahaten's presence. The air inside the room warmed, her racing pulse slowed.

"She's gone now. We're alone."

Josh raised his hand and laid it against her cheek, stroking her lower lip with the gentle caress of this thumb.

"How about you? Do you believe in reincarnation?"

"After what's happened over the past few days, I'm ready to believe in almost anything." As she spoke, she tugged on the hem of her blouse and drew the soft cotton fabric over her head. "I've accepted the fact there are ancient curses, otherworld guardians, and time travel. I don't, however, believe I'm the reincarnated daughter of an ancient queen-Pharaoh."

"It's not totally outside the realm of possibility." Josh grasped the front closure of her bra and slipped the hook from its eye. The satin cups hung loosely against her skin, parting yet not falling from her breasts.

"Anukahaten does have the power to return us home," she told him. "However she hopes we'll stay and search for the statue."

"The decision to stay or go is ours?"

"Yes." She pushed the clingy material aside, freeing her breasts for Josh's gaze, for his touch. "All I have to do is ask."

He sighed deeply and she could tell he was struggling with this latest development. No doubt the father in him wanted to get home to his children. The adventurer likely wanted to stay.

"We're here. I don't see any reason we shouldn't at least try to find the statue."

"You're not worried about your girls?"

"Of course I am. But, I'm also hopeful that whomever, or whatever, brought us here has no intention of causing my family undue heartache. I have to trust they know nothing of our disappearance."

She dropped her bra to the floor atop her shirt and then closed the short distance between them until she straddled his legs. When she raised herself to her knees and pressed her breast to Josh's mouth, he closed his lips around her and pulled her into a gentle suckle.

"I'm agreeable," she confirmed, her words catching on the gasp she drew when Josh nipped at her breast. She would agree to anything, she quickly realized, if it would keep her in Josh's bed.

Josh wasn't certain how he felt about the possibility of being constantly watched by some otherworld guardian. However, he knew he couldn't delay the inevitable much longer. Making love with Teri had quickly become his drug of choice and every minute he spent near her, but not with her, was like an hour without a fix. Even now, with nothing more than her bare breasts to tempt him, he'd become as rigid as the limestone effigies in an ancient noble's tomb.

He wrapped his arms around Teri's waist and stood. Within three long strides, he reached the bed. "Let's hope Anukahaten keeps her promise and leaves us alone."

"Dr. Cain, surely you're not a prude, or shy. At least it wouldn't appear so by the way you described the Egyptian orgies in your book."

As if to dispel her teasing, he stripped Teri's slacks and skimpy panties down her legs, tossing them to the side, leaving her gloriously naked in the middle of the bed. Within seconds, he shed his own clothes and stretched out beside her.

"I'm not shy and definitely not a prude. I'm just not an

exhibitionist. And, as for the descriptive scenes, those were just simple facts."

"Simple facts," she repeated. "They didn't sound so simple to me."

Josh pulled her close to his side, pillowing her head on his shoulder. He tilted her chin up until their gazes met. "Now who's being prudish?"

"I meant to ask you about the comment you made earlier at Mr. Parsket's house. You were saying the etchings on the relief confirmed it belonged to someone close to Tetisheri. What was so special about the etchings?"

"The etchings gave a very vivid description of Tetisheri's and the Pharaoh's love life." He laid his hand against Teri's breast and kneaded her gently. "Tetisheri spoke of the way Sekenenre Tao I would stroke her breasts and how he would suckle at her teat." Josh bent his head and laved her nipple with his tongue before drawing her into his mouth.

"What next?" she asked on a half-whisper, half-whimper. She shifted beneath his touch, as if eager to learn more from the ancient love manual.

"He would kiss his way downward, across the plane of her rounded belly." He followed his words with actions, kissing his way across Teri's midriff, the flat rather than rounded belly, until he'd settled comfortably between her thighs.

"And . . ." Teri prompted.

"And this."

The moment Josh pressed his mouth to her inner thigh an onslaught of tremors coursed through her very core. When he took the first taste, she gasped and threaded her fingers through his hair and spread her legs even further, granting him complete access, begging him without words for the pleasure he'd barely hinted at.

Teri climaxed a half-dozen times before he finally kissed his way back up her body and filled her with his pulsating arousal. Even now, as he lay atop her fully spent, he continued to stroke her, calm her, and draw from her the very last measure of sensual tension.

Teri awoke the next morning to the sound of rain beating against the windows. She opened her eyes slowly, unwilling to let the last remnants of sleep escape. Rolling over, she laid her arm across Josh's waist and snuggled close.

"Good morning," he said softly, his warm breath washing over her cheek.

"Good morning."

"It's late. We're due at the museum in less than an hour."

She shook her head from side to side. "Don't want to get up. Couldn't we play hooky today?"

"'Fraid not, sweetheart. We've got work to do."

In an attempt to change his mind, she ran her hand from his waist, to his chest and back down to his morning arousal. "Are you sure?" she teased. "I'd love to have a private lesson on the sexual habits of ancient Egypt."

"I'll make you a deal." Josh took hold of her stroking hand, removed it from his body, and then slid from the bed. "If you get up, come to the museum with me, and put in the three or four hours we promised Dr. Goodson, I'll tell you all about Neferure when we return to the hotel. Given you might be her reincarnated self, wouldn't you like to know how naughty you were in a past life?"

"I couldn't have been that naughty, or you wouldn't have gotten out of bed."

"Nature calls, my little vixen." When he reached the bathroom doorway, he turned back and added, "And yes, Neferure, you were very, very naughty."

She threw herself back on the bed and stretched out from side to side. Closing her eyes, she imagined what she would do to Josh to show him just how naughty she could truly be.

Chapter 12

"Good morning, you two," Dr. Goodson said, waving them toward where he waited. "I was hoping you'd arrive soon."

"What can we do for you?" Josh asked.

"There's a new shipment of artifacts coming in later today from Professor Henry Sutton. He mentioned you and your wife were his guests for a short while."

"Yes," Josh confirmed. "We spent a couple of days out at his dig site."

"He's bringing in a number of limestone pieces. I'd appreciate your assistance in dating them," Goodson said.

"I'd be happy to help, of course."

Goodson turned to walk back to his office, stopping suddenly to add, "Also, we had the strangest visitor this morning. Definitely not the type of man I'd like to meet in a dark alley. He said to tell you he'd see you later, something in regard to having information on that statue you were asking about."

"Did he say when?"

"No, just that he'd be in contact."

"Thank you. If you don't need us for anything else at the moment, my wife and I will finish up those last two crates from yesterday."

"Good plan," Goodson said. "I'll send my assistant for you when Sutton arrives with the pieces."

Josh led her toward the unrestricted storage room, rather than the workroom where the unopened crates were waiting.

"What are we doing in here?" she asked.

"We need to go through the last of these pieces to make sure none of them belong to Hatshepsut. If we're going to put her tomb to rights, we might as well include everything we can find."

"I agree. After all, she just might be my mother," Teri said, chuckling at the preposterous thought.

"You laugh now, but don't be so sure. Stranger things have happened."

"Not to me, they haven't."

As much as they both hoped to find more artifacts belong to the queen-Pharaoh, it was obviously not meant to be. They'd left the first storeroom an hour earlier and gone to back to the workroom to unpack the remaining boxes.

Teri sat down on the rickety folding chair near the corner of the room, the last of four boxes nearly empty. Josh had gone to meet with the curator and Professor Sutton, leaving her alone in the storeroom.

"You work hard to restore the history of my people."

Anukahaten's softly spoken words drew Teri's attention to the far side of the musty room. An almost ethereal presence floated amid the storage shelves.

"It is the least we can do while we await the discovery of the statue," Teri said, suddenly realizing she was beginning to enjoy these unplanned encounters with her otherworld visitor.

"Your lover's expertise on our culture is most welcome."

"He's not my lover. Well, yes, he is my lover. However, Josh is more than that. He's a learned scholar with a love for your history, your culture and the land and its people, both past and current."

"You admire him," Anukahaten confirmed.

"Yes, very much."

"Then I shall admire him as well." Anukahaten slowly moved her head from side-to-side, as if she were studying Teri's expression. "Do you love this man?"

Teri's heart skipped a beat, the very question setting her emotions on edge. "It's complicated. We're different in so many ways, and both have careers to consider. Plus, let's face it, we've been brought into some extremely strange circumstances. It definitely skews how we would normally feel about one another."

"That does not mean you cannot love."

Rather than continue down a path she was not ready for, Teri changed the subject. "May I ask you something?"

"Yes, of course."

"You called me Neferure before. Do you think I am the reincarnated spirit of Hatshepsut's daughter?"

"It is not what I think, Neferure, it is what I feel."

"But—"

"I must leave you now. I will not return unless you are in danger."

"Danger?"

"If you need me, just call my name and I will come to you. There are many thieves out there who steal the antiquities of my culture. I trust you and your scholar will find Hatshepsut's statue and reunite it with the sacred stone so my queen can finally rest in peace."

"We will do our best," Teri assured her.

A moment later, Anukahaten was gone.

By the time Josh returned for her, Teri had completed the last of her tasks. "I've finished the cataloging," she told him when he came through the door. "Despite being interrupted by Anukahaten."

"She was here?"

"Yes, she admires you for your obvious expertise."

"Really?"

"I'm pretty sure she admires your body too. I mean what red-blooded woman wouldn't?"

"There you go, being naughty again, just like Neferure."

"I asked her whether or not she believed me to be Neferure reincarnated."

"And, what did she say?"

"She said she 'felt' it. She also said she wouldn't be back unless we were in danger. At least she's watching out for us in that regard."

"Better she's on our side of the curse, I suppose."

"Have we heard anything else from this morning's mystery man?" she asked.

"No, nothing. I assume he'll make contact when we return to the hotel." He drew her to her feet and into his arms. "If we're done here, I see no reason to not head back to our room. We'll either meet up with the stranger, or we'll get to that history lesson I promised. Either way, it should be an interesting afternoon."

She pressed her lips to his. When she lifted her head, she agreed. "There's nothing I like better than an interesting afternoon except, maybe, an even more interesting night."

When they arrived at the hotel, the desk clerk called them over. "A note has been left for you, Professor Cain," the man said, handing Josh a simple brown envelope.

"Thank you," Josh responded, taking the offered item from the man's hand and replacing it with a couple of coins.

Gently grasping her arm, he led her toward the staircase for the climb to their room. The moment they were behind closed doors, Josh slipped his fingers beneath the sealed flap and lifted. She peeked over his shoulder, her excitement waning quickly when she realized the message was written in Arabic.

As patiently as she could, she waited while Josh deciphered the note. "Well?" she asked once her patience had hit its limit.

"He claims to have the damaged statue belonging to Hatshepsut. He wants to meet today at four on the far side of town. I have less than twenty minutes to get there."

"Do you believe him?"

"I have to believe he has some knowledge of the piece, given he knows the statue belongs to the queen-Pharaoh." Josh glanced at his watch. "I should be back by five, five-thirty at the latest."

"If you think I'm letting you go alone, you're crazy. I'm coming along. There's safety in numbers."

He chuckled. "If he's a crook, he'll likely have company and his numbers will greatly outweigh the two of us."

When Josh started toward the door, she caught up with him, sliding her hand through the crook of his arm. "Yes, but we have something he doesn't."

"Like what?"

"Anukahaten."

To Teri, this area of the city looked more like the set of a zombie apocalypse movie or, worse, a war zone. Every building was in disrepair, the obvious lack of light inside the dilapidated structures casting an eerie pall over their surroundings. Even the taxi driver had taken off the moment he'd been paid.

"Are you sure this is the place?" she asked.

"It's the number on the note," he assured her. "Here, take my hand and watch your step."

She gladly took Josh's hand in hers, closing her fingers tightly around his. As for watching her step, it seemed nearly impossible to make even the slightest bit of forward progress without encountering broken glass, shattered cement, and every so often, a furry rodent.

Do one thing every day that scares you.

She hadn't realized she'd muttered the quote out loud until Josh responded.

"Eleanor Roosevelt. Smart woman."

"That she was. Book smart and street wise. And, in that vein, couldn't we just wait by the door?"

He held up the note to the last of the vanishing light. "Building Ten, Room Six." Nodding, he said, "It should be just to the left."

"Good afternoon, Dr. Cain," the deep, thickly accented voice beckoned. "And, the lovely Mrs. Cain as well. I am honored by your presence."

Josh turned, placing himself squarely between her and the short, yet dangerous-looking man.

"You have us at a distinct disadvantage," Josh said. "Given we do not know your name."

"You may call me Cecil." Another, much more imposing, man stepped out from the shadows. "This is my friend, Ahmed. He is here to keep me company."

"Do you have the statue?" Josh asked.

"That's what I like, a man who gets right down to business," Cecil said. "I may have the statue, or possibly know of its whereabouts."

"What is it you want for the statue, or its location?" Josh asked.

"Money of course, Dr. Cain. Isn't that why we're all here in Cairo, to become rich by discovering ancient ruins?"

"Some of us prefer to donate the antiquities, rather than sell them." Josh paused, and then asked, "What can you tell me about the statue?"

"Our visit today has little to do with the whereabouts of the statue," he said. "More importantly, do you have the stone that fits in the statue?"

She could sense the tension increasing in Josh's already wary stance, could feel it in the tightening of his grip on her hand.

"I'm not sure what you're talking about," Josh countered. "What stone?"

"Don't be a fool, Dr. Cain. We know you were asking about a statue built to hold a stone. You wouldn't be so eager to find the statue if you didn't possess the stone." Cecil let loose a short, impatient, snort. "So, I repeat, do you have the stone?"

"Not with me," Josh said. "It is locked away at the museum."

"Pity that," Cecil said. "I guess Ahmed and I will have to insist on retaining your wife's charming company until you can retrieve it."

"As I suspected," Josh said, far more calmly than she felt at the moment. "You have no idea where the statue is, do you? Your only interest is in obtaining the stone."

"Let's just say, I couldn't care less about reuniting the stone with its broken idol. However, the stone itself is worth hundreds of thousands of dollars."

"It is?" she asked.

The evil man laughed, the sharp cackle of his voice sending shivers down Teri's back. "I take it you do not share your husband's expertise on the subject of antiquities." Nodding toward his friend, he ordered, "Escort Mrs. Cain into the next room, Ahmed, while Dr. Cain and I discuss business."

Josh released her hand slowly, nodding just slightly in encouragement. "You'll be okay," he told her. "Just do as the man says."

"I don't want to leave you," she insisted. "I'd rather stay—"

The sharp tug on her arm brought her halfway across the room. "Come, lady," Ahmed said, his English barely discernible.

The big man shoved her through the door and into a tiny room, a single chair the only concession to comfort. Rather than sit, she paced the refuse-littered enclosure. Ahmed stepped just outside the door to stand guard.

She could hear raised voices coming from the other room, their argument a mixture of broken English and Arabic. She paced the six-by-six room again, stopping at the door only long enough to make sure the dangerous looking Ahmed remained outside. On her third pass, she tested the stability of the folding chair and lowered herself cautiously onto the cracked seat.

She'd barely settled into place when the sound of a scuffle and breaking wood drew her to her feet and back toward the door. What has Josh thinking? Why would he tangle with such dangerous men?

Ahmed left his post to go to the aid of his partner. Teri thought of following but realized she'd likely be more of a handicap than a help and stood rooted in the doorway, doing her best to see out into the main room. The light had dimmed even more, the lantern Cecil carried now dark.

Another crack of lumber sounded and the shouts of both Cecil and Ahmed echoed through the open space. "Where did he go?" Cecil shouted. "Get the woman."

"Anukahaten, Anukahaten," Teri called.

She could hear both Cecil and Ahmed approaching and she scurried back toward the far corner of the room, hoping to blend into the darkened shadows. A crash sounded, louder than before, and then nothing. She held her breath and waited.

"Teri, are you in here?"

"Josh?"

He stepped into the room, the lantern in his hand, its short wick casting an ominous glow from the doorway to the closest wall. His lip was cut, and had begun to swell.

"Are you crazy?" she said. "Whatever possessed you to pick a fight with that squirrely little man and his pet giant?"

Josh chuckled, the very sound causing him to wince. He pressed his fingertips to his lip and wiped the blood from his fingers onto his dusty jeans.

"Let's get out of here," he told her, leading her back through the door and out the way they'd entered.

"What about Cecil and Ahmed?" she asked.

Josh raised the lantern and swung it in the direction of a pile of loose debris. The two men lay beneath the rubble, crushed by the fallen wall.

"I'd say Anukahaten came through on her promise."

A sudden chill ran down her back and up her arms. "Yes," she said, another rush of the unknown covering her skin in goose bumps. "I guess she did."

Chapter 13

Teri was never so grateful for Josh and his many areas of expertise as she was when he managed to hot-wire Cecil's ancient auto so they could drive back to the hotel rather than walk.

"Are they dead?" she asked when they were on the narrow, rutted road leading into Cairo.

"I didn't stop to check," he said, "but as history's shown us, the other-world guardians rarely leave anyone to tell tales."

The idea Anukahaten might have killed the two thieves on their behalf sent another involuntary shiver down her back.

"What will we do with the car?"

"It would come in handy, no doubt. However, who knows how many shady partners the dear departed Cecil had in his acquaintance. It would be best if we dumped the car before we get to the hotel."

Once they'd made it to the outskirts of Cairo, they parked the car on a deserted side road and walked hand in hand for the last half-mile, the sun slipping below the horizon just as they entered the hotel lobby.

"Dr. Cain," the desk clerk called as they approached, "I have a message for you from a Mr. Donald Parsket."

Josh took the folded paper and thanked the man. "We'd appreciate it if we could have some food brought to our room," Josh said, "whatever the chef has handy will be acceptable along with a bottle of wine."

"I will have everything delivered within thirty minutes," the clerk assured them.

They climbed the stairs, Josh checking the route in front of them as well as behind. His vigilance gave her comfort, a sense of safety. The moment Josh opened the door to their room her much needed safety net collapsed in front of her eyes.

Their room had been ransacked, their few belongings ripped to shreds, the linens torn, the bed tipped over, and the mattress sliced open. The same treatment had been given to the settee in the living area, as well as the two side chairs where they usually sat to eat.

"Stand here by the door with your back to the wall," Josh ordered, "and don't move until I tell you to."

He picked up a broken chair leg and ventured further into the room, checking the closet, beneath the over-turned bed and finally in the bathroom. A moment later, he came to where she waited, an empty container of toothpaste clenched tightly in his hand.

"They even ransacked the bathroom?" she asked in disbelief.

"Right down to emptying the toiletries into the sink," he confirmed.

"The stone, is it truly safe at the museum?"

Josh shook his head. "No, it's not." Patting the front watch pocket of his jeans, he told her, "It's right here, with me. However, given the events of today, perhaps we do need to scout out a safer place for the stone than in our possession."

"The safe deposit box, perhaps, with the money?"

"I'd thought about that," he explained. "On the off chance we were to find the statue, I'd decided it best to have the stone at the ready. I'm second guessing myself now."

"What are we going to do about this mess?" she asked, her gaze scanning what little was left of their room.

"I'll go downstairs and get the manager. I'm sure he'll be more than happy to make this right."

The hotel's manager apologized repeatedly for the state

of their room. "I do not know how this could have happened," he insisted, "or why my staff did not hear such a ruckus."

"We would appreciate being moved to another room," Josh told him. "Perhaps, if it's not too much trouble, we would like one overlooking the gardens, as opposed to the courtyard or the street."

"I will put you on the very top floor in our nicest room," the man explained. "I will have my assistant move your things immediately."

"There aren't any things to move," Teri said, her thoughts going to the clothes Josh had bought for her their first day in Cairo.

"The hotel will gladly replace any necessary items, Mrs. Cain."

"We would appreciate that," she said sincerely.

It was well past midnight when they finally settled into the more opulent room.

"This is nice," she commented, pressing her hand into the thick feather mattress, testing its comfort.

"If I'd known they were going to put us in their best suite," Josh joked, "I might have trashed the room myself."

She laughed, Josh's words drawing the first humorous thought she'd had in hours. "The clothes the hotel purchased for us are very nice."

"Yes, and far more expensive than the ones I'd bought earlier."

She lifted the silk pants and blouse into her hands and fingered the soft material. "Not exactly work attire, especially for the musty storeroom at the museum."

"At least they included another couple pairs of khakis and cotton shirts," he said, removing the remaining items from the edge of the bed and placing them in the closet.

"If we have everything put away, I'm going to take advantage of that huge bathing tub."

Josh crossed the room in a few long strides and peeked into the bathroom. "It is rather roomy, isn't it?"

She smiled and made a show of batting her eyelashes. "Why Dr. Cain, I do like the way you think."

Long after Teri had fallen asleep, Josh lay awake in the big bed, his arms wrapped around her warm, lush body. Despite their hour long, extremely satisfying physical encounter and his undeniable fatigue, Josh couldn't relax. Every nerve ending in his body felt as if it were attached to a battery, the ends of each lead sparking randomly, setting him on edge.

He'd been frantic with worry when the huge thug Ahmed had pulled Teri away from him and shoved her into the tiny room. When he'd taken the swing at Cecil, Josh had silently hoped she'd call on their guardian, Anukahaten, for help,

Ahmed had come running at the first sound of a scuffle, the big man's meaty fist connecting with Josh's jaw, before he'd swung the two-by-four that sent Ahmed sprawling and gave him time to escape among the piles of debris.

He'd never been as grateful for any type of divine intervention as he was when he saw the wall falling down around the men as they made their way in Teri's direction.

He thought back over the events of the day, beginning with their arrival at the museum. Teri had willingly finished their unpacking and cataloging while he'd assisted both the curator and Sutton in dating the limestone reliefs and statues found on Sutton's dig.

Josh had been as discreet as possible when he'd questioned both Sutton and Dr. Goodson on the local collectors and if they knew of anyone who collected broken, incomplete pieces in particular.

He thought back about the note they'd received

from Donald Parsket just before they'd discovered their ransacked hotel room, the man's cryptic message playing over in Josh's mind.

Two statues, neither quite fits the bill. Check them out anyway. Come by for details. D. P.

Somehow Cecil and his trained monkey Ahmed had found out about their quest, whether from someone associated with the museum or, perhaps, because of Parsket's contact on his behalf. Either way, he didn't believe either the curator or the collector were directly behind the robbery attempt.

Josh made himself a mental note to call on Parsket first thing in the morning. He thought of the stone tucked away in the pocket of his worn, dirty jeans, and of how he would keep it safe until they could find the statue. The last of his mental inventory caused him the most concern. He'd foolishly risked Teri's life when he'd taken her with him to the seediest part of town. He needed to protect her as surely as he did the pink stone. However, he doubted she'd agree to stay behind when he went to see Parsket.

She was certainly daring, willingly doing whatever was necessary to accomplish the task before them. He wondered about her visions and Anukahaten's claim that Teri was the reincarnation of Hatshepsut's daughter, Princess Neferure.

Was it possible? Or, was it only a figment of Teri's overstressed imagination?

Teri shifted at his side, snuggling more deeply into his embrace. Her unbound blond tresses tickled his chest, tempting him. His recently satiated flesh sprung to life once again, coaxed into readiness with no more than the glide of her smooth skin against his body. Josh bit back a curse, willed his body to relax, and closed his eyes in search of sleep. His head filled with visions of ancient Egypt, half-finished pyramids, and Teri sitting atop a litter being carried by muscle-bound slaves.

"Neferure," he whispered, his last waking thought that he'd once again forgotten to tell Teri just how naughty she'd been in her supposed previous life.

Teri opened her eyes, the near-blinding brightness of the sun penetrating her closed eyelids and forcing her awake. She stood on a slate floor, two marble columns on each side. Off in the distance she could hear the shouts of men, orders given in an ancient language. She strained to hear what they were saying, surprised by the fact that she understood their every word. More voices rang out with commands to keep moving, followed by what sounded like the crack of a whip.

"Finally I have found you, Neferure. Your mother has been asking for you."

"Excuse me?" She turned toward the sound of the woman's voice, coming face to face with a much younger Anukahaten.

"Our queen-Pharaoh requests your presence in her bedchamber."

"My mother?" she repeated.

"Has this unbearable heat withered your senses, Neferure?"

"No, I am fine."

"Then, come, we should not keep Hatshepsut waiting."

She followed Anukahaten through the narrow corridors, the walls made of dark brown mud bricks, the floor a combination of slate and crushed loose stone. Anukahaten opened two heavy doors and stepped back, allowing Teri to enter ahead of her.

"There you are, daughter. I was beginning to think you had gone off to be with your lovers."

Teri stopped short of the woman's bed, her gaze darting from the supine form laying back amid plush pillows to the scantily clad man at her side cooling her with an oversized feather fan. Across from the foot of the bed there stood a beveled mirror, and she spared a quick glance at her own reflection. What she saw nearly caused her knees to buckle.

She could make out her own image, but in a different form, dressed in ancient garb of silken gowns trimmed with gold threads. Neferure.

"Come sit beside me, daughter. I will soon draw my last breath and I want you by my side when I do."

She sat on the edge of the bed and lifted Hatshepsut's hand into hers. "Is there anything I can do to make you more comfortable?"

"There is little time to worry over comfort. You must leave here as soon as I die. Your stepfather will want you gone and it will be safer for you to leave on your own than by his hand. Promise me you will allow my trusted servant, Anukahaten, to guide you to safety away from this place."

"I promise."

Hatshepsut closed her eyes, settling back into the thick pillows. Moments later, she was gone.

"Come, Neferure, we must do as Hatshepsut asked."

She placed her hand in Anukahaten's and followed the woman out of Hatshepsut's bedchamber.

"Where are we going?"

"Follow me," Anukahaten said, leading them down a dark passageway. "It is through here we will make our escape."

The distant sound of Josh's voice penetrated Teri's panic. "No, not there," she whispered. She pushed at his chest and tried break free of his grasp.

"Sweetheart, wake up. You're having a bad dream."

She opened her eyes and blinked once, twice, seeking clear focus. She laid her hand against Josh's cheek.

"Josh."

"Good morning. That must have been some dream you were having."

She shook her head. "Not a dream, at least I don't think it was a dream."

"Then what was it?" he asked, pulling her into a tight embrace.

"I'm not sure. I was in ancient Egypt and I could understand the language. There were slaves building a new temple for Tuthmosis III. I saw Anukahaten and Hatshepsut. I saw my own reflection but it wasn't me, it was Neferure."

He smoothed his hand across her cheek, her brow, pushing aside her sleep-tangled hair until he could stroke the silky column of her throat with his fingertips. "What else did you see?"

"I was there, at her bedside, when Hatshepsut died."

She raised her head and pressed her lips to his. He returned the kiss with one of his own. "Then what happened?"

"Hatshepsut said I had to escape or face danger at the hands of the Pharaoh Tuthmosis so I let Anukahaten lead me away from the temple. We were going down a long corridor similar to the one we came through when we first arrived in this place and time. I was afraid she was taking me back without you. I begged her to stop, to let me come back to get you."

"It's over, Teri. You're here, I'm here. Everything's fine."

She trembled, her body reverberating in his arms.

"Make love to me, Josh."

Josh skimmed his fingertips across her throat, her shoulder, and down through the valley between her breasts. He slid his hand lower, across the plane of her stomach and threaded his fingers through the short thatch of hair at the very apex of her thighs.

Against her ear, he whispered, "It would be my pleasure, Neferure."

Teri closed her eyes and relaxed back into the comfort of the big bed, the feel of Josh's hands on her body causing every inch of her skin to tingle with arousal. He slid his finger inside her, retreating and advancing in a slow lazy rhythm.

Her hips rose and fell of their own accord, seeking a deeper penetration. Still, he teased her, playing the edge of her arousal like a fine instrument, drawing one orgasm after another, causing her breath to come in short, staccato puffs, her pulse to race like a finely tuned sports car.

"Josh, please," she begged, certain she'd burst if he didn't take her completely.

He slid his hand forward, slipping two fingers into her hot, needy core, drawing yet another release with the very first stroke. He began again, pushing forward, retreating, and filling her completely with the slick glide of his fingers until she came again, and again, and again.

She reached for him, needing more than just the stroke of his fingers, wanting him buried as deeply as possible inside her body.

"You're becoming impatient, my love," he teased.

"Yes, I am."

She wiggled from beneath Josh's warm body and pushed him backward onto the bed. She took his rock-hard erection in her hand, sliding her palm across his length, teasing him as he'd done her. His breath caught when she bent forward and took him into her mouth.

She settled comfortably between his legs until she could stroke him in the same, aggravatingly slow increments he'd used on her. Josh wound his fingers through her hair and cupped her head in his grasp, guiding her.

There was something heady, arousing about providing your lover with oral stimulation, she realized. Closing her eyes, she went about the task of seduction with renewed vigor, with the desire to bring Josh to the very edge of sensual insanity.

"Enough," he gasped, the ragged sound of his voice

sending her over the edge, drawing yet another climax from deep within her body.

She raised her head and met Josh's glassy gaze. She smiled at him, and then ran her tongue along the length of his shaft before making her way up his body and straddling his hips. Slowly, she lowered herself over his erection, reveling in the feel of him as he filled her one satisfying inch at a time. Teri leaned forward until she could whisper in his ear, "I love it when you're buried so deeply inside me there's nowhere else for either of us to go."

He groaned and shifted beneath her, raising his hips, setting her in motion, urging her to finish what they'd started.

Gladly, she acquiesced to his request.

Chapter 14

Their hired car pulled up in front of Donald Parsket's home at half-past ten, the driver accepting the fare with a quick tip of his cap.

Josh stepped out onto the driveway and offered her his hand.

"I'm glad you decided to bring me with you," she said. "I don't like being alone in the hotel, especially after what happened yesterday."

"Parsket's place is as safe as any, maybe safer. He has more than adequate security."

"He'd have to, given the value of his collection," Teri noted. "I'm not an expert like you but I'd bet these artifacts are worth at least a million dollars."

He drew her hand to his lips for an all-too-brief kiss. "Most likely closer to three million but who's counting?"

She stood at Josh's side and waited for Parsket's butler to answer their knock. Barely more than a minute passed before the door swung open to allow them inside.

"Welcome back Dr. and Mrs. Cain," Ariel Parsket said, joining them in the entryway. "My husband will be with us shortly if you'd like to take a seat in the library."

"Thank you," Josh acknowledged, offering the older woman his arm and taking Teri by the hand.

"Donald was able to locate another collector who specializes in statues, both limestone and ivory. However, as he said in his message to you, he doesn't believe either of the two statues he was able to view are what you're looking for.

That's not to say, of course, that there might be others that would fit the bill."

"I assumed by his request for our visit he has additional information," Josh said. "Otherwise, the message wouldn't have been necessary at all."

Before Mrs. Parsket could answer, the door opened and Donald Parsket arrived by way of wheelchair, his valet pushing him to where they waited.

"Mr. Parsket." Josh held out his hand in greeting and the older man clasped it in his own.

"Dr. Cain, I'm glad you could make it. I understand you've not had any luck finding the elusive statue."

"We thought we had one lead but it turned out to be a false alarm."

"That false alarm wouldn't have anything to do with the two bodies they found over in the old grain mill, would it?"

Josh only shrugged. "Not that I'm aware of. Cairo can be a rough place if you cross the wrong person, I suppose."

"And, Mrs. Cain," Parsket began, turning in her direction. "How are you enjoying your first trip to Egypt?"

"I'm getting used to the heat finally," she told him. "And, I've developed a fondness for dates."

"That's a lovely outfit you're wearing," Ariel commented.

Teri ran her fingertips across the hem of the silk blouse before saying, "Thank you. It's handmade from one of the shops in the marketplace next to our hotel."

"Rumor has it, your hotel room was ransacked," Parsket said.

"It's not a rumor, I'm afraid," Josh confirmed. "I can't imagine what the thieves would have been looking for given I sold our only item of value to you."

The older man nodded, but didn't comment.

"I've asked the maid to bring iced tea," Ariel said.

"Thank you," Teri replied.

"What can you tell us about the statues you saw?" Josh asked.

"Both were badly chipped, one made of limestone and the other an inferior grade of ivory. I estimated their origin to be mid-to-late twentieth dynasty, nowhere near the age you're looking for. However, I also spoke with a man, a Phillip Durning, he's an archaeologist from somewhere in the States. He's working out on a dig with another man, a Seth Tupper. Tupper apparently is from the southern states somewhere, but spends at least half the year here in Egypt and owns a home just outside Cairo. Durning says Tupper is fascinated with anything ivory, and that the man has a fairly extensive collection of ivory statues."

"Where can I find this Tupper fellow?" Josh asked.

"He's got a registered dig about five miles past the third Great Pyramid. Both he and Durning went out this morning. It doesn't appear as if they've found much of value so far, but I'm sure a man of your expertise might prove useful to their expedition."

"Unfortunately, we're without transportation. I'll need to go back to the hotel and—"

"I assumed as much," Parsket said, interrupting. "That's why I have a business proposition for you, Dr. Cain."

"A proposition?"

"I will provide you with one of my vehicles as well as supplies. In exchange, I will get first look at anything of value you might procure along the way."

"And, if Tupper doesn't allow me on his dig?" Josh asked.

Parsket shrugged. "You win some, Dr. Cain, and you lose some. I'm a gambling man and, to me, you look like a pretty safe bet."

"I plan to leave at first light. And, I'd really rather you stay here," Josh admitted. Gathering up a couple pairs of khaki shorts and a handful of cotton shirts, he stuffed everything into an old leather satchel he'd borrowed from Donald Parsket. Along with a work-battered truck, a tent, and camp supplies.

She shook her head, gathering up her own clothes and shoving them in beside Josh's things. "There is no way you are going back out in that desert and leaving me here alone. No way."

"Even with the supplies Parsket gave us, we aren't guaranteed a spot among Tupper's camp. If we have to pitch our tent away from the rest of the group, I can't guarantee your safety."

"I'm not worried. I trust Anukahaten will keep her word and protect us."

"What will you do while I'm underground, assuming I'm allowed?"

"Perhaps I can help Mr. Tupper the way I did Professor Sutton. Maybe I'll even be able to sound him out on the statue. My questions will sound like idle chitchat and possibly put the man off guard whereas he might be leery of your interest given your level of expertise."

"As much as I hate to admit it, you might be onto something."

"And just why would you hate to admit that, Dr. Cain?"

Josh pulled her into his arms. Raising her chin with the lightweight touch of his fingertips, he met her gaze. "Because I wasn't the one who thought of it, of course."

The moment the sun set, Josh took her hand in his and drew her toward the huge bed in the center of the room, stopping just short of the edge of the thick feather mattress. With the gentle brush of his hands, he pushed her blouse up and over her head. Kneeling in front of her, he slid the silky pants down her legs, taking her satin panties in the same sweep of his hand. When she stood naked before him, he urged her back onto the bed before stripping himself of his shirt, jeans, and boxers.

"We've got an early day tomorrow," he reminded her.

She held out her arms in welcome invitation. "Then, Professor, I'd suggest you come to bed so we can get some sleep."

Josh shook his head and took his place at her side. "Sleep is for the weak."

She chuckled, drawing him to her for a slow, wet kiss, before adding, "And highly overrated."

They were up an hour before dawn. The truck packed, they left Cairo just as the sun broke the horizon.

"How will we know when we've come to the right location?" she asked.

"Legally, there has to be at least three miles between each dig," Josh explained. "So, if we start from the third pyramid and drive five miles, we should be at the right place. Assuming, of course, Parsket's information was correct."

"Donald Parsket doesn't impress me as the type of man who receives or shares incorrect information."

"He certainly has his pulse on everything happening in and around Cairo," Josh conceded. "Not a bad thing if you're in the business of collecting."

They drove for what seemed like hours, the old Model T a far cry from the speedier cars she was used to. "I have the overwhelming urge to cry, 'Are we there yet?'" she said, laughing.

"Try to stifle that urge please. I hear it enough when I travel with my . . . with . . ." Josh's words stuck in his throat.

She stretched her arm across the width of the truck's front seat and laid her hand on his, stroking the back of his wrist with her fingertips, a gesture meant to soothe rather than incite.

"I'm sure your daughters are fine, Josh. No matter what's happened back home, they know you love them and that you'll come back to them as soon as you can."

"We've been here for over a week, Teri. What if time is passing at the same rate there? They'll be frantic with worry."

"We can go home if you'd like," she reminded him. "All we have to do is ask and Anukahaten will send us back."

He shook his head yet she could see the angst in his drawn expression, the pain in his eyes. "Three, four more days tops, that's all I'm willing to give. I need to get home to my children."

She patted his arm and smiled, an offering of understanding and support. "If we don't find the statue by the weekend, we'll ask to go home."

"We could leave the stone here," he suggested, "and then come back in our own time to look for the statue."

"Do you really think we'd find it? Even if some collector has it now, who's to say we'll be able to track it down nearly one hundred years later. I say we give it our all now, in this place and time, and if we fail, we call on Anukahaten to keep her word and let us go."

Josh pulled the truck to a halt at the end of a man-made access road. Pointing off in the distance, he told her, "I'm pretty sure that's Tupper's camp."

"Then let's go introduce ourselves, Professor."

Josh turned onto the narrow access way and steered the truck toward the center of the encampment, his strong grip on the steering wheel the only thing keeping the truck level on the uneven road. Once he pulled to a halt, he opened his door and climbed down from the running board, landing on the ground in a cloud of dust. Teri followed closely behind.

"Hello," he said to the man walking in their direction. "I'm Dr. Joshua Cain, Princeton University. Donald Parsket said you might be in need of an extra pair of hands and some additional expertise."

"You the fellow who worked on Sutton's dig for a few days?" the man asked.

"Yes, I am."

The man stuck out his hand. "Tupper, Seth Tupper." Nodding toward where Teri waited, he asked, "Is this your wife, Dr. Cain?"

"Yes," Josh confirmed. "It's her first trip to Egypt so she's full of questions. However, she's a hard worker. She did some cataloging for Sutton if you're in need of assistance."

"Nope, got that covered. My daughter and grandson are with me. Millie was brought up on dig sites. She handles the cataloging. I'm sure she'd welcome the company though. It can get pretty lonely for a woman out here, especially while the men are down on the dig."

"How old is your grandson?" Josh asked.

"Four and already interested in becoming an archaeologist like his grandpa."

"It's good to get them interested when they're young," Josh said.

She could tell by the wistful look on Josh's face, he was thinking of his daughters again and likely wishing he'd never seen the *Eye of the Pharaoh*.

"If you want to join us for coffee," Tupper said, "we can discuss an honorarium for your work."

"I was thinking more along the lines of one of the pieces from the find. Like any collector, owning a piece of history is far more interesting to me than money."

"Do you have a favorite type of item? Reliefs? Urns?"

"Statues actually," Josh said. "Limestone, ivory, marble."

"And you, Mrs. Cain, what have you seen that strikes your fancy?"

She shrugged. "Personally, I like anything gilded in gold, or stones, the bigger the better."

The older man let out a hearty laugh. "Let's get that

coffee. I've got a fair collection of statues myself, Dr. Cain. Perhaps you'd like to see them while you're in Cairo."

"I'd enjoy that very much," Josh said. "Thank you."

They followed Tupper into the largest of the assembled tents and toward a grouping of narrow tables. An auburn-haired woman hovered over a young boy, encouraging him to eat his breakfast.

Another man sat at the table farthest from the boy. Tupper led them in the man's direction.

"Dr. Joshua Cain, Mrs. Cain, my associate Phillip Durning," Tupper said, nodding in the man's direction.

Josh held out his hand. "Nice to meet you, Durning."

After the briefest of pauses, Durning shook Josh's hand. "I'd heard there was another American archaeologist in town," he confirmed. "Professor Sutton claims you were responsible for quite the find over on his dig."

"We did all right."

"Why didn't you go back to Sutton's camp?" During asked. "I'm sure he would have welcomed you with open arms."

Josh shrugged. "There's not likely much left to find. I thought I'd offer my assistance at a new site, maybe see if I can help scare up some additional places to search."

"It does seem to be what you're good at, Dr. Cain," Seth Tupper added. "Sutton said it was almost as if you can sniff out those hidden chambers."

Teri thought briefly of the advantage Josh had over the two men across from them, his knowledge of what had already happened providing him information the other man have yet to glean for themselves.

"This is my daughter, Millie Stevens," Tupper said as the young woman approached, "and that little rascal fussing over his cereal is my grandson Huck."

Teri extended her hand to Millie. "It's nice to meet you, Millie. I'm Teri."

"Welcome, Teri, it'll be nice to have some female company for a change."

"Huck?" Teri repeated, a smile tugging relentlessly at the corners of her mouth.

"Pops insisted we name him after Huckleberry Finn, his favorite fictional character."

Chapter 15

Within the hour, the men were ready to depart for the dig. As it always did, her apprehension grew the moment Josh strapped on his equipment belt and hardhat.

"You be careful," she said softly. Laying her hand against Josh's chest, she raised herself onto her tiptoes and pressed her lips to his for a quick kiss.

Josh nuzzled beneath the curtain of her hair and whispered, "You take care of our little pink bundle."

When he stepped back, Teri patted the front pocket of her jeans, assuring him with no more than the nod of her head that the *Eye* was safe in her possession.

Josh, Tupper, Durning, and two hired diggers started up the rise leading toward the entrance to the dig, Millie and Huck following behind. Teri quickened her steps to catch up with the other woman.

"I walk my grandpa to the big hole every day," Huck announced proudly when she caught up with them.

"You do?" she responded, her tone teasingly light.

"I'm gonna be an arcologist when I grow up."

She ruffled Huck's blond bangs, telling him, "I'll just bet you are, and a really good one at that."

"We go as far as the edge of the rise," Millie explained. "Huck has rules to follow if he wants to be allowed on the site, don't you Huck?"

"Yes, ma'am. No going near the opening to grandpa's dig, no going near the air holes, and no playing in the deep sand."

"Air holes?" Teri asked.

"The ventilation shafts." Millie pointed off to the left of the site. "See the red flag. It marks where they've dug narrow shafts to help with ventilation in the dig site." She moved her arm to the right. "There's another one there and then there's a third on the opposite side of the site."

Once they'd come to the edge of the entranceway, Huck raised his hand and waved to his grandpa. Tupper waved back. A moment later, the men moved out of sight.

From their vantage point on higher ground, she turned full circle and took in the surroundings. Sand, mounds and mounds of sand, for as far as the eye could see.

"There, off in the distance," Teri said, pointing to their left. "What is that?"

Millie shaded her eyes and squinted. "It looks like the markings from a previous dig. Most likely, it's the boundary marker designating the edge of their registered site."

"I thought the sites had to be at least three miles apart."

"That's right. The measurement is taken from the center of one dig to the center of the next dig. However, whatever site was there is no longer a working dig, so the three-mile rule doesn't apply. That marker looks to be less than an eighth of a mile away, so we're likely right up on the edge of the abandoned site."

"Hopefully that doesn't mean there's nothing for the men to find. I'd hate to think they were working so hard for nothing."

"Sometimes the difference between finding a hidden chamber and coming up empty handed is a matter of a few hundred feet, just as your husband discovered over on Professor Sutton's site."

"You enjoy this, don't you?" Teri couldn't help but feel an admiration for Millie and her willingness to brave the hot sun and scorching sand in support of her father's ambitions.

"It's what I grew up on. Every summer after school

ended, we'd leave the States, come here, and dig. I met my husband here on one of my father's digs."

"Is your husband still involved?" Teri asked, hoping her question wasn't too personal.

"Yes, he'll be arriving at the end of the month. He teaches history at the University of Florida, but spends his summers here with dad. Huck and I came over a bit early to help with the setup."

"I'm sure you will be happy to see him."

"I'll be happy to have his help corralling Huck. He's always begging to go down onto the site but, until Trevor gets here to keep an eye on him, I dare not let him go."

"An extra pair of hands will be great, I'm sure," Teri agreed.

"Actually, a few extra pairs of hands. Trevor is bringing some of his students with him. There'll be six of them eventually working both the site, and the loose digs around the area."

"Loose digs?" She winced at the thought of yet another unfamiliar term.

"They're surface excavations, in and around sand dunes, at the edges of old sites. It's amazing the things you can find buried just a few feet beneath the sand."

"Bones," Huck said, adding to their conversation. "Grandpa says you can find bones."

Bones. Teri wondered if Tupper, Durning, Trevor Stevens, and his students would be the six men to find the remains of the high priest and Pharaoh's guard who had stolen the *Eye* from Hatshepsut's tomb. Hopefully, without the stone there to be discovered, none of the six men would face the original outcome . . . a certain and untimely death.

Josh crossed the width of the empty chamber and back again, studying the walls, running his hands across the scraggily surface in search of any sign of an opening, any crack in the hard rock. Off in the distance, Tupper and Durning were chipping away at an outcropping of limestone.

The diggers toiled against one wall, their efforts widening the chamber's surface, but not disturbing the stability of the dig.

Josh came to a stop at Tupper's side, his gaze drawn to the area where the man worked.

"What's your assessment of the site, Dr. Cain?"

"There doesn't seem to be any false walls. However, once we've cleared this last limestone deposit, we could find something. These wall markings indicate a presence in the chamber. However, they appear to be a twenty-first dynasty dialect, not nearly as old as you were hoping."

"I'll take twenty-first dynasty," Durning added, "At least we've found some indication we're digging in the right place, or at least close."

"Sometimes it's only a matter of a few feet," Josh said in agreement. "We just haven't hit the edge of those few feet as yet."

The three men worked side-by-side for the next few hours, uncovering little more than a few pieces of pottery and a wooden vessel. Josh held the chipped remains of a twenty-first dynasty bowl against the light of the brightest lantern. "My best estimation is we've stumbled upon a servant's quarters."

Durning shifted from one foot to the other, scanning the items they'd found. "Not much for a half-day's work, but better than nothing."

"Especially if the noble he served is close by," Tupper added. "What say we go topside for some lunch and fresh air and then come back and get started on the area the diggers have uncovered."

"Sounds like a good plan to me," Josh agreed. Hoisting his canteen in the air, he added, "I could use a drink of water not laced with silt from the dig."

The moment they arrived above ground, he went in search of Teri, the need to see her, assure himself of her safety even more important than the water he'd requested.

She was his water, he realized, his relief from the dirt and the heat, and he wanted nothing more than to draw her into his arms and revel in the feel of her soft curves and the taste of her sweet mouth.

"There you are," he said, approaching the table where Teri sat.

He'd no sooner spoken when she rose from the chair and launched herself into his arms. "You're back, safe and sound," she said, relief evident in her tone.

Josh drew her into his arms and held her tightly to his chest. "Yes, I'm back, at least for a couple of hours." He pressed his lips to hers and filled his senses with her minty flavor.

"You two must be newlyweds," Millie commented, coming up behind where they stood.

"It's that obvious?" Teri asked.

"Six months," Josh said. "And still in love."

Josh willingly absorbed the tiny tremor that shook Teri's body when he'd uttered the simple lie. He tightened his embrace and met her gaze when she lifted her head. She smiled up at him and his heart jumped into his throat.

"Assuming, of course, he keeps his promise and gets me back to the States before I shrivel up from this heat," Teri joked.

"It's definitely not for everyone," Millie admitted. "You'd think the heat would sweat a few inches off this body of mine." Patting her rather ample hips, Millie added, "Must be my love for the food, especially the honey-laced desserts."

After lunch, both Durning and Tupper went into the storage tent to drop off their meager discoveries which, according to Seth Tupper, were barely worth cataloging. Millie left the main tent to put Huck down for a much-needed nap.

"We've about an hour, maybe less, before we go below again," Josh commented. "Care to take a little rest with your husband."

"A bit of alone time would be nice," she admitted, "given that we're newlyweds."

Josh took her hand and led her toward their tent. Once inside, he removed his shirt and used the basin of tepid water to wash away some of the dust from the morning's search before stretching out on the camp bed set up in the corner. "Care to join me?" he asked when he'd settled in.

"To rest," Teri clarified, "nothing more." She stretched out at Josh's side and pillowed her head on his shoulder.

Immediately, he slid his hand beneath the hem of her cotton shirt and enclosed her breast in his hand. "Are you sure?"

"Yes, I'm sure. You need your rest if you're going to go back for another few hours of digging."

He opened his mouth, as if he intended to disagree. Yet, when she gave a gentle push to his shoulder, he settled back and closed his eyes.

Teri propped herself on her elbow, content to watch Josh sleep. She'd never known anyone like him. Intelligent, caring, a generous, thoughtful lover. The perfect package. And, for the time being, hers.

Unfortunately, Josh's much-needed sleep was rudely interrupted all too soon by the blaring of a car horn. He opened his eyes and dragged his palm across his face, rearranging his fatigue.

"Tupper?" she guessed.

"Yep, time to get back to work."

While Josh donned a clean shirt, Teri asked, "So, what did you find this morning?"

"Not much. A servants' quarters by the look of it. Twenty-first dynasty, most likely, which does provide me with a bit of information which may come in handy."

"Really, like what?" she asked.

"Most often, the servants' quarters were added on as an afterthought once the noble's temple was complete, so they were found on the south side of the dig. If we go another five hundred feet or so to the north, we could uncover another chamber."

"That would take you close to the previous excavation site."

"Yes, it would."

"Is it possible whoever dug at the other site already uncovered the tomb of the noble and then didn't bother with the servant's quarters?"

"It's possible, but not likely. I have a feeling if there are any tombs of significance out there, they'll likely be about halfway between where we're digging and where the last group finished."

"Are you going to tell Tupper what you think?"

"I may have to," Josh conceded, buttoning his shirt and walking to the front of the tent. "We need something to take back to Parsket. And, we'll need a bargaining chip if we're going to get a look at Tupper's collection of statues."

"Nothing makes a man like Tupper more grateful than helping him discover a trove of ancient ruins," she guessed.

"Agreed. I'd bet the only thing more important to Seth Tupper is his family."

Chapter 16

"I envy you," Millie said once Teri had taken her seat in the main tent.

"Why?"

"Young and in love. I can't remember the last time my husband looked at me the way Josh looks at you."

Teri quickly pushed aside the thought that Josh truly loved her. Obviously, they were both better actors than they'd given themselves credit for, at least to Millie.

"How long have you been married?" Teri asked.

"Fifteen years, give or take a century." Glancing over to the corner where Huck played, she added, "I thought we'd never have a family. We were always traveling from one site to another, one country to another. Trevor never wanted children. He said they'd only be in the way of our work. His work, my father's work."

"I'd say your father disagrees. Huck seems to be the light of his life."

"After my mother died, Dad went on a work-bender, traveling all over the world in search of ancient ruins, anything and everything to get him away from his home in South Carolina. He never came back to the States until just before Huck was born. He stayed with us in Florida for six months. At first I thought it was to be near his only grandchild. Then, I realized he was exhausted. He'd about traveled himself to death."

"He seems fine now," Teri pointed out.

"Yes, he only travels about half the year now. He's here

from April to October. Trevor and I usually join him after school ends and then return home at the end of August."

"But this year, you came early with your dad."

"Yes," Millie confirmed. "It's Huck's last summer before he starts school, so we thought we'd make it a bit longer for him. Plus, of course, Trevor's busy giving final exams and grading papers and packing for his own trip over. And since he's bringing some of his students, he's helping them get ready as well."

"Well, it won't be long and you'll all be together again."

"Yes, both Huck and I are looking forward to it," Millie agreed.

As she'd done before, Teri couldn't help but feel compassion for Josh and his concern for his family. She thought of her own family and wondered if either her social-climbing mother or workaholic father would even realize she was missing.

Josh surveyed the area uncovered earlier that morning by the two diggers. Tupper stood at his side while he hunkered down and ran his hands along the rough floor of the chamber.

"What do you think? Any chance this is more than just an empty chamber?" Tupper asked.

Josh closed his eyes briefly, indecision clouding his thoughts. When he rose to his feet, he turned in Tupper's direction and shook his head. "What I think is that we're going about this all wrong."

"How so?" Durning asked, coming up to join the two of them.

"If this is late twenty-first dynasty, as I suspect, their burial habits were far different than previous dynasties. They believed in the servants digging their own burial spots after the noble's tomb had been completed and sometimes not until after the noble was already dead."

"And?" Tupper prompted.

"Since most burial chambers are built as far to the north of the pyramid line as possible, it stands to reason the servants' burial site is to the south of their master's tomb." Josh took the compass from his shirt pocket and held it flat in his palm. "I say we need to dig in that direction."

"Aaron Blake, the English archaeologist, already cleared the site north of here," Durning reminded them. "Little more than a year ago."

"What if he stopped too soon?" Tupper asked.

Josh voiced his agreement. "My thoughts exactly. We should start by marking off a spot about halfway in between his southern-most stake and this site and start digging there."

"It's getting late," Tupper said. "Why don't we pace it off in the morning? I'll send one of the men into Cairo to bring back a few more diggers and we'll get started as soon as they arrive."

"We should spend the last couple of hours clearing this chamber of anything of value and then start closing it up," Josh suggested. "The diggers could start by filing in the ventilation shafts."

The three of them worked for another two hours sweeping through the rubble and hand-clearing anything of importance. All the time they worked, Josh mulled over the wisdom of his decision.

Surely the outcome of their quest, their final goal, was important enough to encourage Tupper and his group to extend their search.

What if you're wrong? What if there's nothing to be found? He shook off the taunt of his conscience, wanting more than anything to finish what they started so they could finally go home knowing they'd done everything they could to help Hatshepsut rest in peace.

They arrived above ground just before sunset, Teri,

Millie, and an obviously impatient Huck waiting at the bottom of the ridge.

Josh removed the heavy leather tool belt from around his waist and handed it to a worker who waited patiently to accept the cast off equipment from all three men.

"Why were the diggers filling in the ventilation holes earlier?" Millie questioned.

"Are we quitting, Grandpa?" Huck asked.

"No, Huck, we're only moving a few hundred feet in that direction," Tupper said, pointing toward the older excavation site.

Durning came down the sloped walkway and stopped at Tupper's side. "Dr. Cain seems to think we'll have better luck a few hundred feet to the north."

"And you don't agree?" Millie asked.

Durning shrugged. "I'm not against it. Heaven knows we weren't finding anything where we were."

Josh clasped Teri's hand in his and they started off toward their tent.

"Supper will be ready in half an hour," Millie called after them.

"We'll be there," he confirmed. "I'm starving."

The moment they stepped through the tent flap, he drew Teri into his arms and buried his head against her shoulder and pressed his lips to her throat.

"You decided to tell them," she said softly, attuned to his internal struggle.

"I didn't see any way past it. I knew the moment I saw the area the diggers had uncovered earlier we were in the wrong spot."

"I'm sure you did the right thing, Josh. You always do."

He raised her chin with his fingertips, drawing her to him for a kiss. "I wish I had as much faith in my decision as you seem to."

"You are my lifeline, Josh, my strength in this strange place and time. I trust in your decisions and in your ability to find the statue and get us home safely."

Supper that evening consisted of the standard dried meats and fruit, bread, and the usual bottle of wine. What she wouldn't give, Teri realized, for a cool, crisp salad and a glass of anything non-alcoholic that included ice.

"I'll help with the dishes," she offered, standing to clear the plates and take them to where Millie had set up a bucket of warm water.

"I can wash, if you'd like to dry," the other woman responded, handing her a woven tea towel.

"What are they doing out there?" Teri asked.

"Measuring the distance between the two sites and trying to determine the best spot to start digging the ventilation shafts first thing in the morning."

"Huck was excited at the thought of being able to tag along," Teri added.

"Yes, he's taken a real liking to your husband, especially Josh's willingness to hoist him up on his shoulders and carry him up the steep incline and onto the ridge."

Teri didn't comment, the thought of how much Josh must miss his girls and of how much he worried about them, bringing yet another tightening to her throat, making speech nearly impossible.

Once the men had returned to camp, they spent the next two hours drawing out their plans on pieces of draft paper, using the squares to mark off areas for exploration. She did her best to catch a glimpse of their sketches, work out in her own head exactly what would transpire over the next day or two while they opened yet another site in the middle of the desert.

She thought briefly of Anukahaten, and of Hatshepsut and what it must have been like to live in a place such as this. If she closed her eyes, the memories of her brief dream, her vision of herself as Neferure, came quickly into her thoughts, the images vivid in her head.

"You look lost in thought," Millie said, a clean dish balanced on her outstretched hand.

"Sorry," Teri responded, taking the tin plate from Millie's grasp and running the towel across the flat surface. "I must have been daydreaming."

"They're lost in conversation over there," Millie explained, nodding toward where the men worked. "If you don't mind finishing up here, I'll go make a pot of coffee. They'll probably want to sit up for a while yet and plan out their strategy."

"Sure. You go ahead."

The moment she'd finished the last of the dishes and put the linens away, Teri excused herself and went back to their tent.

Once there, she removed her sweat-stained clothes, bathed in the lukewarm water from the pitcher and bowl beside their bed, and then climbed beneath the lightweight blanket and relaxed back onto the pillow.

Despite his promise to be along shortly, at least an hour, maybe two, had passed before Josh entered the tent. As she'd done, he stripped out of his clothes, washed quickly at the basin, and then slid into bed at her side.

"You're still awake," he said, drawing her into his arms.

"I was replaying the day over and over in my head," she admitted.

"And?"

"Did you know Millie's husband was scheduled to arrive at the end of the month?" she asked.

"Tupper mentioned something about it. Apparently his

son-in-law isn't much for chamber digs, but prefers to comb the surface for treasures."

"He's bringing three students with him for the trip."

"Tupper didn't mention anyone other than Millie's husband, Trevor."

"That'll make six, Josh. Six men, some of whom will be combing the sand for whatever they can find." She paused then asked, "Do you think they might be the six who find the priest and guard's bodies?"

"I suppose it's a possibility. The timing is about right."

"And, given that we have the stone, do you think history has changed and they'll be spared the horrible deaths mentioned in the stories of the curse?"

"Again, another possibility. There'd be no reason for the curse to take them if they're not in possession of the *Eye*."

"Are we certain the priests and guards didn't take the statue at the same time they took the stone?"

"The reports were inconclusive. It's a fact I've wondered about myself over the past few days."

"What if the priests and guards took the statue too? What if, the statue is still buried out there somewhere in the desert and was found originally with the stone intact?"

"If that were the case, then the statue and the *Eye* would have never been separated."

"What do you think, Josh?" She laid her hand against his cheek and pulled his gaze in her direction. "What's your expert opinion?"

"If you take the accounts of the curse literally, the stone was the only thing Akhenaten was after. His intention was to place the stone in a gold idol for Nefertiti. There was no need for the statue, so I firmly believe it was left behind and then scavenged by grave robbers prior to Cook's original discovery in 1902."

"Then that's what I believe too. Now, let's just hope

Tupper has the statue as part of his vast collection. And, that we can find a way to make him part with it."

"Let's keep our fingers crossed that my hunch on this new site pays off," Josh said, a yawn drawing out his words.

"Enough talk, Professor," she teased, snuggling more deeply into Josh's strong embrace. "It's time for some sleep."

"But, what about—"

She pressed her fingertips lightly against his lips, stilling his words.

"Sleep, Josh. You've got an even bigger day ahead of you tomorrow."

Chapter 17

"*This way, Neferure, before the Pharaoh's guard finds us.*"

Teri took Anukahaten's outstretched hand and followed her down the long corridor. How had she gotten back here? Was she asleep, or having another vision?

"*Where are we going?*"

Anukahaten tugged on her hand, pulling her along. "*I am taking you to the high priest's temple. It is the last place the Pharaoh's guards will look.*"

"*What about the high priest? Does he not serve the Pharaoh?*"

"*He does, but his servants do not. They despise both men and will gladly hide you in one of the many rooms among the temple walls.*"

"*I don't understand. Why am I in danger? Surely I pose no threat to Tuthmosis III. After all, he is my half-brother.*"

"*Which is why he wishes to see you dead. He wants to sever all ties to your mother. And, erase—*"

"*All signs of a queen-Pharaoh among the family's lineage,*" Teri finished, remembering Josh's words from the research he'd uncovered back in New Orleans.

"*Yes. He believes it destroys his hold on Egypt and weakens his reign.*"

"*I can't stay hidden forever,*" she pointed out. "*Where will I go?*"

"*I am not sure,*" Anukahaten confessed, "*I only know that I will keep you safe, as I promised my queen.*"

She followed Anukahaten along another corridor until they'd reached the very bowels of the huge temple. Servants *scurried around them, barely raising their heads to register the unusual arrival of the late queen-Pharaoh's daughter and her guardian.*

"When will you come back for me?" Teri asked.

"As swiftly I can, Neferure," Anukahaten promised. "I must first lead the Pharaoh's guards away from this place."

They came to a small room, its contents minimal. "This is where you're leaving me?" Teri asked.

"Until the sun sets, then we will make our way across to the temple."

She'd barely taken a seat on the bed in the corner of the room when she heard the sound of loud voices coming in her direction. She jumped from the bed and moved to the darkened corner of the room.

"Along here," the man shouted, "I'm sure they came this way."

"Teri, wake up. You're having another dream." The calming sound of Josh's voice pulled her back to reality. She opened her eyes, rolled onto her side, and buried her face in the crook of his shoulder.

"I was there again," she said softly. "With Anukahaten and running away from the Pharaoh's guards. She was taking me to safety. She thought I was Neferure."

Josh drew her close and raised her chin with the gentle touch of his hand, meeting her gaze. "You were Neferure, at least in that place and time."

She shook her head. "No, I couldn't be."

He pressed a kiss to her brow and settled more deeply into the bed. She placed her hand against his chest and felt the even rhythm of his heartbeat. The steady cadence relaxed her and she released a long sigh.

"Since we're both awake, why don't I tell you a little bit about your former self?" Josh suggested. "We have at least a half hour before dawn."

"Even the naughty parts?"

"Perhaps we'll save those for later, when we're back in the seclusion of our hotel room."

"You really know how to spoil a girl's fun, Professor."

Josh chuckled and then began, "First of all your, or should I say Neferure's, history is one of the most clouded in all of Egyptian history. There have been many conflicting stories about how long Neferure lived. Some researchers believe she died before her mother, Hatshepsut. Some believe she was present at her mother's burial. Some say she married her half-brother, Tuthmosis III and bore his first son."

"Perhaps that's why Hatshepsut wanted me hidden. Anukahaten believed he wanted to kill me, but maybe what he wanted was an heir."

"I can't say that I blame him for wanting to get you into his bed." Josh teased.

She swatted playfully at his shoulder then stroked her fingers along the length of his forearm and back again. "What else do we know, or not know, about my supposed previous life?"

"During Hatshepsut's reign as queen-Pharaoh, Neferure took on the role of Princess and held many titles, among them Lady of Upper and Lower Egypt, Mistress of the Lands, and God's Wife of Amun, a title previously held by Hatshepsut before she declared herself queen-Pharaoh. Despite her tender age, Neferure represented the royal family with grace."

"The first time I saw myself as Neferure, before Hatshepsut died, she made a strange comment. She said she assumed I'd been with my lovers. Just exactly how many 'lovers' did I have?"

"Again, there are conflicting reports. Some believe you took a lover as early as age ten, and that you were the sexual prodigy of your tutors. There's even a statue of you and your first tutor, Senenmut. Neferure is sitting on his lap and covered by his robe. Very suggestive, if the scholars are to be believed."

"Ten?"

Josh chuckled. "You have to remember, it was a very different culture than we have today. Brothers and sisters married, mothers married their stepsons, girls became wives as young as age six, and women became mothers as soon as they were physically able to reproduce."

"Suddenly, I no longer feel guilty about giving my virginity to Bobby Collins after homecoming at the ripe old age of seventeen."

"As you shouldn't. It was yours to give."

She slid her hand from Josh's chest to his morning arousal, taking him fully in her grasp. "If we've got another fifteen minutes before the sun comes up, I wouldn't mind sharing a bit of my wanton past."

They'd barely finished breakfast when the truck returned with six additional diggers to help excavate the new site. Two men began on the ventilation shafts while the rest started on the site opening. Teri found herself impressed with the efficiency of the entire operation, each man working like a cog in a well-oiled piece of machinery. Of course, seeing Josh working in the hot sun, devoid of his shirt, his bronzed muscles gleaming with hard-earned sweat was enough to make any job impressive.

Her hands tingled with the thought of sliding her palms across Josh's slick skin, of raking her fingers through the fine hairs on his chest, and feeling his muscles tighten beneath the smooth glide of her touch.

"Your husband is a hard worker," Millie said, "I know my father appreciates his help." Nodding to the other side of the work site, she added, "Mr. Durning prefers to supervise."

"Your father is quite impressive for a man his age as well," Teri commented. "He's working right alongside the others."

"Yes, you'd think he'd start to slow down at some point. However, the thrill of discovery is Dad's adrenaline. It definitely works better than caffeine."

"Is Huck down for a nap?" she asked.

"For the time being," Millie confirmed. "He's almost to the age where naps are no longer necessary. I'm hoping he'll hold out until it's time to start school."

She helped Millie fill an enormous water container and lift it onto the wooden sled. Together, the two women pulled the entire apparatus up the sandy incline, stopping just a few feet short of where the men worked.

Josh put down his shovel and came to take the offered drink of water from Teri's outstretched hand. "Thank you," he said, leaning forward to press a kiss to her cheek.

"You're welcome. How is the excavation going?"

"Slow but steady. We've located what looks to be a pathway. Once we've uncovered it a bit more, we'll be able to tell if we've stumbled on a new site or one that's already been discovered and then re-buried by the ever-shifting sand."

"So, you were right to move the dig to between the two sites?"

"It would seem so," Josh said.

No doubt he felt it was a bit too early to toot his own horn. For a brilliant man, his modesty never ceased to amaze her.

He was about to set aside his tin cup when Seth Tupper came to join them. "Your husband is a genius, Mrs. Cain. I'd have never thought to measure out a center point between the two outer markers."

She laid her hand against Josh's forearm and raised her gaze to meet Tupper's. "I've always thought so, Mr. Tupper. But, then again, I might be the slightest bit prejudice."

"Let's not get ahead of ourselves," Josh warned, his tone filled with caution. "We could be digging up an abandoned site, already emptied of its contents."

"That's the name of the game, my boy," Seth said, slapping Josh on the back. "Over the course of thirty years, I've had far more busts than I've had successes."

"Why do you keeping looking?" Teri asked, sincerely wanting to know.

"Because when you make that one find, that one pristine discovery, it's worth its weight in gold, if not in money then in pure satisfaction."

"Spoken like a true lover of the hunt," Durning said, walking up to join them. "However, I prefer to be a bit more practical. You're quite welcome to the satisfaction, Seth. I'll take the money any day."

Josh returned to where they were clearing away the sand on the top of the ridge. Somewhere amid the drifts and dunes they should find an opening, a set of mud block stairs leading downward into a chamber.

He turned around and raised his hand to shade his eyes from the afternoon sun, studying the landscape, assuring himself of the location from nothing more than memory. He felt a bit apprehensive, almost ashamed, of the advantage he had in the search. He had to keep reminding himself it was for the greater good.

He thought about Seth Tupper and, as Durning had said, his true love for the hunt. He had no problem helping Tupper unearth what could prove to be a very lucrative dig. There was something about Durning that gave him pause. He didn't trust the man.

Josh scanned their surroundings a second time, and then a third. Tupper worked off to his left, his enthusiasm more than making up for what the older man lacked in muscle.

Durning, as usual, stood off to the side, leaning on his shovel, pushing the sand around with the toe of his boot, pretending to be busy when, in fact, he'd not lifted more than a bucketful of sand the entire day.

The urge to talk to Tupper privately, to encourage him to end his partnership with Durning was first and foremost in Josh's thoughts. Yet, it wasn't his place.

His place was back in the States, teaching at Princeton, being a good father to his daughters. Spending time with Teri. The last thought caught him off guard. Over the course of the past eight days, she'd become more to him than just his publicist, his publisher's babysitter, and a great lover. She'd become his partner in what was quickly becoming the strangest, most compelling, adventure of his life.

It was just past sunset when the workers called it a day. The three ventilation holes in place, the opening to what promised to be a new site less than a hundred feet from their grasp, Teri waited patiently while the men took their seats at the communal dinner table.

"This looks good." Josh pushed the wilted greens aside in favor of a toasted slice of unleavened bread and piece of perfectly cooked lamb.

"Millie taught me how to make camp bread," Teri admitted, lifting a piece to her lips. "Let's hope it tastes as good as it smells."

He took a bite of the flat, warm bread. Closing his eyes, he sighed deeply, as if savoring the saltiness of the spices, the slight tang of the lemon butter she'd spread across the top.

"You're obviously a fast learner," he said, opening his eyes to meet her gaze. "It's delicious."

While the men planned their strategy for the next morning, Teri helped Millie clear away the dishes. Huck had placed himself squarely between his grandfather and Josh and hung like an eager student on their every word.

"He's really engrossed in their discussion."

Millie chuckled. "He doesn't understand all of it, but he does try to follow along. I know Trevor is looking forward to the day when they can work side-by-side."

"When does your husband arrive again?" Teri asked.

"He leaves the States the last weekend of May and should arrive here late that Sunday."

Teri closed her eyes for a moment, briefly reviewing the calendar she'd committed to memory just before they'd left Princeton. The last weekend of the month would be Memorial Day, and they were scheduled to be in Chicago. As both she and Josh had done on numerous occasions over the past week, she wondered whether or not time was moving forward without them.

Josh came up behind her, slipping his hand through hers and pulling her toward the path to their tent. "If you'll all excuse us," he said, "we're heading to our tent. Sunrise, and those last hundred feet, are not too far away."

"Night, you two," Millie called out.

"Goodnight, Millie," Teri said in return.

They'd barely gotten to the tent, when Josh asked, "Did you enjoy watching the excavation process?"

"I enjoyed watching you work, especially the part where you took your shirt off."

He shook his head and drew her into his arms. "There you go again, Neferure, being a temptress."

Toying with the buttons on the front of his shirt, she shot him a coy smile. "Exactly how many lovers did I have in my rather short life span?"

"Altogether, or at the same time?"

"At the same time?"

"As I'm sure you've gathered from the numerous depictions on the limestone steles we unpacked at the museum, orgies were a common occurrence. Just because you were the daughter of a queen doesn't preclude you from taking part."

"I suppose not. However, in this lifetime, I think I'll stick to one man at a time."

"Just men?" he asked, a mischievous grin lighting up his face. "That doesn't sound much like you, Neferure."

She raised her hands up in a show of playful defeat. "That's enough for tonight. I'm willing to wait until we're back in Cairo, or better yet, back in our own place and time, before I delve into the naughty nuances of my previous life."

Josh stripped out of his clothes, then used the water basin and hand-formed soap to wash away the worst of the day's dust before slipping naked between the sheets. "Coming to bed, my little vixen?"

"I might as well," she conceded, pulling the cotton shirt over her head and dropping her shorts and underwear to the ground. "There doesn't seem to be an orgy in sight."

Chapter 18

Teri could tell by the raucous shouts of the workers that they'd breeched the entrance to the site. She and Millie made their way along the road until they stood just below the newly discovered opening. Huck, as excited as the men seemed to be, tugged restlessly at his mother's hand.

"Can I go, Momma?" he pleaded. "I wanna see what Grandpa's found."

"Wait here until your grandpa comes to get you. You know the rules."

Huck nodded, his full-lipped pout tugging on Teri's heartstrings.

"Does your father take Huck underground?" Teri asked.

"If the site is safe, he'll take him down and let him look around before they start excavating. Once they start digging, there's always the threat of a wall collapse, so he's not allowed inside the chamber from that point on."

Teri shaded her eyes and scanned the top of the slope, as impatient as Huck for some indication of what they'd discovered.

"Come on up, Huck," Seth Tupper shouted, "I'll take you down for a quick look-see."

Huck scrambled up the side of the site as fast as his short legs could carry him. "Coming, Grandpa," he hollered. "Wait for me."

Tupper and Huck disappeared over the rise.

Teri was about to turn away when Josh called out. "Would you ladies like a guided tour?"

The thought of setting foot inside a centuries-old tomb had her scaling the pathway as fast as little Huck had just moments earlier. "Are you coming, Millie?"

"No thank you," Millie responded, turning toward camp. "I grew up on excavation sites. Once you've seen one, you've seen them all."

"You might be surprised," Josh said, his words stopping Millie in her tracks.

"Really," Millie asked. "It's not just another servant's quarters?"

"No, it's not."

As fast as Teri was moving, Millie beat her to the top of the rise. Moments later, they were descending centuries old stairs and stepping into an ancient, but completely intact, room.

"You're awfully quiet. Are you okay?" Josh asked, draping his arm over Teri's shoulder.

"Yes," she said softly. She turned full circle inside the vast chamber, barely able to believe her eyes. "I don't know what to say. I'm speechless."

"We've come upon a pre-burial chamber, most likely late nineteenth, early twentieth dynasty," Josh explained, ushering her forward with the gentle nudge of his hand. "Over here we have the preparation area, complete with tools for removing the organs prior to mummification."

He bent over and lifted a circular, dirt-crusted vessel into his hands.

"What was that used for?"

"Most likely it was placed below the work table to catch any remaining fluids as they drained from the body."

She cringed. Her slight shiver caught Josh's eye and he chuckled. Leaning close, she whispered, "Creepy."

"Here," he said, pulling her to the left, "are scraps of linen, used in the wrapping process and extremely well preserved."

"If this is the preparation chamber, where would the actual tomb be located?"

Josh tipped his head, indicating an area to his left. "Through there. Although, depending on the importance of the inhabitant, the wall could be anywhere from six inches to a foot thick."

"The thicker the walls, the more important the person?" she guessed.

"Something like that," he said. "We'll start cleaning the surfaces down as soon as you, Millie, and Huck are safely topside. Once we get a look at the wall etchings, we'll be able to figure out who we're dealing with, or at least the importance of the burial site."

"Tupper looks happy with his find."

"As well he should be. This could turn out to be a major site. There were over fifty tombs uncovered in the early 1920s, mostly of high priests and short reigning rulers. With any luck, this is the burial site of at least a high priest or better."

Their tour lasted a good half-hour with Josh pointing out everything of significance not requiring excavation. Teri and Millie were about to take Huck by the hand and leave when the sound of Tupper's excited call drew them to the far side of the chamber.

"Josh," Seth called out, "over here."

Josh led the way, she, Millie, and Huck close on his heels. Tupper and Durning had cleared away some loose debris and come upon a limestone stele. Josh withdrew the horsehair brush hanging on his tool belt, dropped to one knee, and gently dusted away the first layer of dirt.

"This depiction suggests the tomb of a consort to Setnakhte, the first Pharaoh of the twentieth dynasty. However, if you look at the writings here along the edge, they appear to have been rubbed out, as if the tomb originally belonged to someone else and was cleared and given to a member of Setnakhte's followers."

"Is it possible," Tupper asked, "that the Pharaoh's chamber is nearby?"

Teri could tell by the expression on Josh's face he was pulling up information from his vast bank of internal knowledge. She held her breath in anticipation of what he might say.

"I suppose it's possible, however, unlikely. From the research I've reviewed since Carter's numerous discoveries from 1900 through 1902, most of the twentieth dynasty Pharaoh's tombs have been found in the Valley of the Kings. We're about ten miles south of there."

Tupper turned to his daughter and grandson. "Josh, Phillip, and I are going to stay down here for a while. I'm anxious to uncover the writing on this limestone. You three need to get back to camp." Taking Millie's hand in his, he told her, "I intend to keep you busy cataloging over the next few days. You might want to get your supplies in order."

"Your father seems very excited over the find," Teri commented as she, Millie and Huck climbed the stairs to the opening of the excavation.

"He's had a dry spell these last two years, for sure. It'll be nice to see him enjoying himself again, no matter the value of the discovery."

Despite his protests, Huck went down for his nap. As soon as he was tucked into his camp cot, Mille returned to the main tent.

"Did you need some help getting ready for cataloging?"

"I could use a hand unpacking everything. I would have done it sooner but Dad thinks it's bad luck to set up before he actually has something to record."

Teri smiled broadly at her new friend. "As I've quickly discovered, there are far too many superstitions surrounding ancient Egypt to take a chance." Nudging Millie forward, she added, "Come on let's get those boxes unpacked and everything ready."

The men came up from the dig later than usual, preferring to skip dinner in favor of finding more treasures. With the help of two of the diggers, they carried a makeshift canvas sling filled with a half-dozen items unearthed from the tomb.

"There are sandwiches," Millie said, pointing to the nearby table, "and lukewarm tea, if you fellows are hungry."

"Maybe in a bit, sweetheart," Tupper said. "I'm anxious to get to these items in the last of the daylight and see what else we can decipher."

Teri watched from a distance as they laid out the limestone stele she'd seen in the chamber, a number of mud-plaster reliefs, two canopic jars, and a handful of tools used in the burial process.

As he'd done before, Josh used his brushes to remove the worst of the surface dirt on the first of the three reliefs. Durning spent his time studying the canopic jars. Obviously not on a level with Josh's expertise, she wondered if the man's credentials as an archaeologist were legitimate.

"We'll post a guard on the entranceway," Tupper said, "and then start fresh in the morning. I'm anxious to finish cleaning the inside wall."

"I agree," Josh said. "We're losing light and don't want to make a mistake in the location of the second chamber."

"If you had to put a value on what we've found, Dr. Cain," Durning asked, "what would be your best estimate?"

Josh sat back on the campstool and turned, surveying the items spread out before him. "In some cases, the value is intrinsic. You can set a price as high or as low as you want. However, it all comes down to what the collector is willing to pay."

"Well said, my boy," Tupper agreed. "Well said."

Teri watched the play of expressions crossing both Durning's and Josh's faces. She could almost see the dollar signs in Durning's eyes. The only thing she saw in Josh's expression was mistrust.

She went back to the tent ahead of Josh, her thoughts on the different emotions she could see in each man's response to their day's work. As Josh had uncovered each item and offered his expert opinion, Durning's excitement had grown, the dollar signs she'd seen before multiplying with each of Josh's assessments.

Tupper, on the other hand, was totally oblivious to his partner's greed, enjoying the history and the beauty of their find.

Josh's emotions, although more guarded, surely echoed her own. Caution where Durning was concerned and the desire to protect Tupper from his money-hungry partner.

She poured water into the basin and went through her nightly ritual wishing, as she had on the two previous nights, for the huge claw-foot tub back in their hotel room. Slipping out of the remainder of her clothes, she donned a simple cotton shirt and climbed into bed.

"Your lover has very kind words for our culture, Neferure."

"Anukahaten," Teri whispered. She opened her eyes and scanned the tent from one side to the next, not the least bit surprised when there was no one there. "I wasn't expecting to hear from you again unless we were in danger." A chill ran down her arms despite the intense heat. "We aren't, are we?"

"No. You are safe for the time being. Does your lover—"

"His name is Joshua," she said, wanting Josh to be thought of more for his expertise than for the fact they were lovers.

"Joshua," Anukahaten repeated. "He is wary of the man with the beard, is he not?"

"We both are. He's greedy and only sees these treasures for what they will bring him."

"Yet, Joshua shares with him. Why?"

"He is business partners with the other man, a good man. We believe Mr. Tupper may possess Hatshepsut's statue so we are willing to help him so we can see his collection and ascertain if he does, in fact, have what we're looking for."

"And, if he does? How will you get it from him?"

"We'll offer to buy it, or ask for it as payment for the work Josh has done here at this site. Without Josh's knowledge, Mr. Tupper and his partner Mr. Durning would not have found the chamber."

"Barter, it was often the way of my people."

"Yes, I know. I am slowly coming to understand and appreciate the culture, as Josh does."

"I will go now," Anukahaten told her, "but I will be nearby if you need me."

"Thank you."

Josh came into the tent at that moment, a chuckle preceding his words. "You're welcome. For what I'm not sure, but welcome all the same."

"I was talking to Anukahaten, not you." The ease with which she accepted such a strange occurrence drew another of Josh's deep laughs.

"Did your visitor have anything of importance to relay?"

"She doesn't trust Durning."

"Well, she can get on the bandwagon for that one. The man's a weasel."

"That he is."

"I'm sorry we took so long. Tupper had a hard time deciding how best to protect his pieces until Millie was able to catalog and pack them in the morning."

"And, what was his decision?"

"They're stored in his tent, beneath his camp cot. Likely, he's sleeping with one eye open and a shotgun across his lap."

She lifted the lightweight cover, inviting Josh to join her. "Why don't you get out of those clothes and join me? Let's see what we can lay across your lap, Dr. Cain."

Chapter 19

The men were ready to return to the dig site shortly after dawn, barely stopping for breakfast and coffee. Teri helped fill the canteens and handed them out as each man left the tent. Four of the diggers had been paid and left just after breakfast, leaving only Josh, Tupper, Durning, and two of the stronger men to help with the heavy work.

She poured herself a second cup of coffee and took a seat between Millie and Huck. "So, Huck, what do you have planned for today?"

"Nuthin' much," the boy said, a frown rearranging his chubby cheeks. "Grandpa won't let me help him and mommy's got work to do."

"You and I could do something," she suggested.

"Like what?"

"Perhaps we could look for beetle shells."

Huck shook his head. "Naw, I think I'll just color in my books and maybe build a fort in the sand."

"I'm a pretty good fort builder if you'd like some help."

He sighed deeply. It seemed obvious that, without the excitement of the dig, even a four-year-old could get bored.

"If you want to," he said finally.

"Don't feel as if you have to entertain my son," Millie told her. "He's got plenty of things he can do. I brought along some coloring books. He's got enough toys to fill a toy store and I've also printed some letters and numbers for him to copy. He starts school in September, he needs to be prepared."

"Is there something I can help you with?" Teri asked.

"I'm going to set up my work table. You could give me a hand moving the pieces they found yesterday."

"Anything you need," Teri said. "I'm willing to help in any way I can."

She and Millie worked side-by-side to get the cataloging area up and working. Carefully, they moved each artifact to the huge table in the middle of the main tent.

"What's this?" Huck asked, poking his finger into a crease in one of the reliefs.

"Don't be touching," Millie warned. "You know what your grandpa says about keeping your hands to yourself."

"I want somethin' to do," he complained.

Millie ruffled her son's hair. "If you want to take your toy cars and trucks out in front of the tent you can, but don't go anywhere I can't see or hear you. Understood?"

"Yes, ma'am."

"And wear your hat so you don't get sunburned."

"Yes, ma'am."

She and Millie worked diligently at organizing the dozen or so items Josh, Tupper, and Durning had unearthed the day before. As she'd done at Sutton's site, Teri manned the logbooks while Millie gave the descriptions. Then, together, they boxed the items one piece at a time.

"That's the last one," Millie said, dusting her hands against her dirt-brown khakis. "All Dad has to do is place his mark on the boxes and we'll be ready to take them back to Cairo."

"What happens to everything then?"

"Dad, Phillip, and now Josh as well will go through everything, date and authenticate each item, and then set an asking price. If there's a specific piece either of them is partial to, it will be considered part of their stake."

"I don't believe Josh has any intention of being a full partner in this. He's only here to help and we likely won't be staying for the duration of the excavation."

"He's considered a partner up until he leaves. It's just the way things work. After that the proceeds become fifty-fifty between my father and Mr. Durning," Millie explained.

"How well do you know Durning?" Teri asked. More important than Millie's direct answer was the expression she could see on the woman's face. A frown creased the corners of Millie's mouth and Teri suspected Millie had the same concerns both she and Josh shared.

"He's worked with my father a few times on previous digs. He's the moneyman I'd guess you'd say, providing more upfront cash for the supplies and diggers' wages. Then, he takes back his investment and they split the remaining proceeds."

"He does seem extremely focused on the monetary value of each piece."

"Durning wasn't crazy about the idea of adding your husband to the team. Had it not been for Professor Sutton's raving about Josh's expertise, he would have likely not agreed. I'm sure now that Josh has made this significant discovery, Phillip is more than happy to have you here."

"We're happy to be here, for as long as we can stay."

"I'd better get Huck in here for some lunch," Millie said, "then get him started on his books and letters."

Mille had no sooner stepped outside the tent when a child's blood-curdling scream echoed through the campsite, bouncing off the tents and sand dunes.

"Huck!" Millie called out. "Where are you?"

Teri was through the door of the tent and at Millie's side in seconds. "It sounds as if his scream came from that direction," she said, pointing toward the original dig site. "Would he go back there to play?"

"No, he knows better than to venture away from the tents."

Millie started off in the direction of the old site while Teri scaled the walkway toward the new dig. "I'm going for help. See if you can get Huck to call out so we can follow the sound of his voice."

"Huck!" Millie yelled as loudly as she could.

"Momma," Huck responded, his voice faint and muffled.

Teri scrambled across the top of the dig site and down the ancient stone stairs leading to the chamber. "Josh, where are you?"

"What are you doing here?" he asked, meeting her at the foot of the stairs.

"Something's happened to Huck. We can hear his screams but we're not sure where they're coming from. It sounds as if they may be coming from just over the ridge on the old site."

She turned and ran up the chamber stairs, Josh and Seth Tupper following in her wake.

"You stay along the road below the site," Josh told her. "Seth and I will circle around from the back."

"Where's Mr. Durning?" she asked. "We could use his help."

"We thought he was with you and Millie," Tupper said. "He was complaining about a headache."

"We haven't seen him all day," she said. "Should I go see if he's in his tent?"

"No, leave him be," Josh said. "If he's sick, he won't be of much use out in the hot sun. The last thing we need is two crises on our hands."

"Millie!" Tupper called. "Huck!"

She searched the road line, as Josh had instructed, stopping at every mound of loose sand in case Huck had gotten stuck under a shifting dune.

Josh and Tupper carefully circled the site while Millie stood in the middle of the original excavation calling her son's name.

Minutes passed, and Teri's apprehension grew with each of Millie's frantic calls. After what seemed like hours, Teri heard the reassuring sound of Josh's voice.

"I've found him," Josh hollered, "over here at the south vent shaft."

Teri arrived first, followed by Millie and Tupper. Josh was stretched out on the ground and looking down into the fifteen-foot drop.

"Why the hell wasn't this filled up like I ordered?" Tupper screamed, lowering himself onto the ground beside Josh.

"It must of have been missed by the diggers," Josh guessed. "Still, there should have been a marker designating the danger of the surrounding ground."

"Can you see him?" Millie asked.

"Yes, he's at the bottom of the shaft. He's moving, but just barely," Tupper confirmed.

"How will we get him out?" Teri asked.

"I'm not sure yet," Josh said. "It will all depend on whether or not he's able to tie a rope around his waist so we can haul him up."

"Why can't someone go down after him?" Millie asked.

"There's not enough room," Tupper explained. "The opening is the widest part but the shaft narrows to barely more than two feet wide as it reaches the ten to fifteen foot depth."

"Is there any way to widen it, or get to it from inside the chamber?" Teri asked.

"Both scenarios would almost ensure a cave-in," Josh explained. "Our best hope is that he'll regain consciousness and be able to put his arms through a harness we'll fashion out of rope."

"Aren't there rescue plans for something like this?" Millie asked, her words vibrating with worry.

"The holes are dug purposely narrow to prevent someone from falling in," Tupper said. "Of course nobody ever expected a child to be playing near a dig site."

"He shouldn't have been here," Millie said, her voice cracking. "He's never left the front of the tent before."

"He's a curious little boy," Tupper said, standing up to wrap his arms around his daughter. "That's my fault. I shouldn't have put such thoughts of adventure in his head until he was old enough to understand the dangers."

"It's nobody's fault," Teri said, hoping to console them both. "Accidents happen. What we need now is a plan in case Huck's not able to help himself."

"Mommy." The sound of Huck's voice, muffled with tears, sent both Millie and Tupper to the ground over the hole.

"I'm here, sweetie. Mommy's here."

"My arm hurts and my foot's bent funny."

"I'm going after some rope," Josh told them. "You two keep him talking. See if you can figure out how badly he's injured."

"Huck," Seth Tupper called out. "Can you stand up?"

"No. It hurts."

"Huck, sweetie," Millie coaxed. "Can you try and stand on one foot maybe?"

"Like when I'm playing hopscotch?" he asked.

"Yes, sweetie, just like that."

The echo of Huck's grunts and groans as he did his best to struggle to his feet tore at every one of Teri's heartstrings. When he began to cry, she felt the first of her own tears well up in her eyes.

"Okay, got the rope," Josh said, stretching out on the ground beside Tupper. "Here, point this light directly into the hole."

Tupper took the long handled flashlight and pointed it toward his grandson.

"Huck, it's Josh. If I lower a rope down to you, can you put it around your waist?"

"No," Huck said. "I can't. I tried to stand up like mommy asked but I couldn't."

"We'll pretend you're a fireman," Josh coaxed, "and you're saving someone from inside a big hole. Can you try?"

"Okay," he said.

Josh slowly lowered the harness he'd made into the hole. "Huck, once the rope gets to you, you'll need to put it over your head and around your waist. Once you've got that done, you tell me and I'll tighten the rope from up here."

"I can see him," Tupper said. "The rope is dangling just above his head. Lower it a bit more."

The pull on the rope meant Huck was doing his best to wrap it around his waist and Terri breathed a sigh of relief.

"I can't!" Huck called out, his sobs starting anew. "My arm hurts too much and my hand's all tickly."

Josh leaned back and pulled the rope from inside the hole. "We'll have to think of something else."

Millie wiped the tears from her cheeks and positioned herself over the hole so she could see her son. "Mommy's not going anywhere, sweetie. You just sit back down and try not to move your leg or your arm. Grandpa and Josh are going to figure out how to get you out of there as quickly as we can."

While Josh and Tupper stood off to one side discussing other options, Teri joined Millie on the ground and looked down into the hole.

"Hey there, Huck," she said, doing her best to make her tone light. "I'm looking forward to building that sand fort we talked about."

"Me too," he said. "I thought that was what me and Mr. Phil were gonna do when we came up here."

"You came up here with Mr. Durning?" Teri asked.

"Yep, he said he found some sand castles to show me."

"Josh," Teri said, turning in his direction.

"I heard," Josh said. "You three wait here."

A moment later, Josh was scrambling down the access road and headed toward the main tent.

"That explains why Huck left camp," Tupper said. "Durning lured him away."

"But why?" Millie asked, a fresh round of tears clouding her eyes.

"My guess," Teri said, glancing off toward the main tent, "is he needed a distraction."

"Son of a bitch," Tupper said, jumping up from his prone position. "If that bastard's endangered my grandson's life just so he could steal from me, I'll kill him with my bare hands."

"Daddy," Millie said, taking her father's hand, "stay here, with me and Huck. Let Durning have whatever he wants. It's not as important as your family."

Tupper collapsed on the ground beside his daughter. "You're right, Millie, as always."

Josh returned less than ten minutes later.

"He cleaned everything out of the big tent as well as the pieces we'd set by the chamber stairs to bring up at midday. He's taken the car and the keys for the truck."

"How will we get out of here with the truck disabled?" Millie asked.

"I can take care of that," Josh assured her. "But first we need to get Huck out of that hole before the sun starts to set."

"I have an idea," Teri said. "I'm not sure it will work, but it's a chance."

"Anything," Millie said.

Teri turned toward Josh. "You said there was approximately a two-foot clearance, right?"

"Yes, maybe a bit more near the top."

"I'm small enough. I can fit through the hole. You can lower me down and I can put the rope around Huck so we can pull him up."

Josh shook his head. "It won't work. There's no room for you to stand once you're down there."

"I don't plan on standing." She paused for a moment before explaining, "Lower me down head first. I can put the rope around Huck like a harness and then you can pull us both back up at the same time."

"It's too dangerous," Josh argued.

"I can't ask you to do that," Millie said softly. "If you were to get stuck or injured, I would never forgive myself."

"We have no choice," Teri countered.

"It just might work," Tupper suggested, coming to Teri's side. A look of concern, mixed with a sense of relief, filled his expressive face.

Teri laid her hand against Tupper's sun-weathered arm. "We have to try."

"I can't believe I'm even considering this," Josh grumbled. Turning to Tupper, he suggested, "Go get the two diggers from inside the chamber. We'll need all the muscle we can get just to pull them both back up safely. I'll go get some more rope and another flashlight."

Chapter 20

"We're coming down to get you, baby," Millie said. "You sit there and be a brave little man."

"I'm hungry," Huck complained. "And I gotta go to the bathroom."

His innocent claims drew Millie's chuckle, the first sign of relief they'd had since the entire ordeal began.

Once Teri was tied off in her harness, Josh handed her the smaller one he'd fashioned for Huck.

"If at any time you feel it getting tight, tug on the guide rope like I showed you," Josh explained. "The last thing we want is for you to brush against the sides hard enough to cause a cave in."

"I understand."

"Once you get Huck into the harness, you'll have to cross his arms over his chest, no matter how much it might hurt his injured arm and hand. There'll likely be tears to deal with," Josh reminded her.

"No doubt," she agreed. "And not just from Huck."

Josh cradled her cheek in his hand. "Are you sure about this?"

"Yes, I am."

Millie stepped forward and drew Teri into a hug. "Thank you."

"Thank me when both Huck and I are back above ground."

Millie shook her head. "Thank you for even trying. It's more than I could ask of anyone."

Josh brushed a quick kiss to Teri's cheek and then turned

her toward the open vent shaft. "Let's do this before I change my mind."

Josh, Tupper, and the two diggers each took a firm grip on the ropes anchoring Teri to her harness. She positioned herself flat on the ground and slid slowly forward until she could see into the hole. Drawing a breath for strength, she leaned into the opening and wiggled her way across the lip of the shaft until she was waist deep into the narrow space.

"Lower me a bit more."

"Is your flashlight on?" Tupper asked. "Can you see Huck?"

"The light is on and I can make out the top of his head," she confirmed.

"Once you're totally inside the shaft, we'll stop lowering you until you're accustomed to being upside down," Josh explained. "It won't do for you to become disoriented."

"I understand."

The moment all motion stopped, she closed her eyes and let a measure of calmness wash over her, through her.

It's all about finding the calm in the chaos.

Drawing a few deep drafts of air, Teri slowed her breathing.

"Mommy?" Huck called out.

"No, Huck, it's Teri. I'm coming down to get you."

"Where's Mommy and Grandpa?" he asked.

"They're above ground waiting for us to be pulled to safety. You'll have to do exactly as I say. Okay?"

"Yes. My arm and foot hurt lots."

"I know they do, but we're going to fix them too. As a matter of fact, we're going to wrap you up like one of Grandpa's mummies."

"Don't wanna be a mummy."

"It's only pretend," she assured him. "And we're going to wrap you with ropes, not linen cloth, so you'll be able to see everything."

Tugging on the center guide rope, she signaled her readiness to keep going. Within a ragged heartbeat, she was being lowered at a slow and steady pace. Once she'd reached Huck, she tugged twice on the rope, the signal Josh had indicated would stop her forward progress.

"Which leg hurts?"

Huck tapped lightly on his right knee. "This one."

"Okay, I'm going to put that one through the harness first. It's going to hurt a little, but I'll be as careful as I can."

She carefully raised Huck's leg only enough to secure the harness before wrapping it around his hips and then the other leg. Tears ran down his dirty cheeks but he didn't let out a sound, a fact for which she was very grateful.

"Now, I'm going to do the same with your arms. Which one hurts the most?' she asked.

"This one," he said, using his left hand to point to his right arm.

She wrapped the next piece of the harness around Huck's right arm first and then his left. Finally, she took the two loose pieces of rope and bound them around Huck's arms and chest and around his legs as far down as she could reach given the limited amount of room.

"Last thing," she said, wiping her hand across his cheeks to remove the worst of his tears. "You need to remain as still as you can while they're bringing us up. Can you do that?"

"Yes, ma'am."

She tugged on the lead rope, telling Josh and the others they were ready to be pulled to safety. The moment they began to move, Huck cried out in pain.

"I'm sorry," she whispered. "It's not going to be easy but we can't help you until we're out of this hole."

Her eyes filled with tears. Another idea came to her, a way of possibly relieving the pressure on Huck's already sore limbs. Quickly, she tugged on the rope twice and their upward momentum stopped.

"Are you okay?" Josh called to her.

"We're fine," she shouted back. "I want to change the position of my hands."

"Remember," Josh cautioned, "you can't let your arms go outside the width of your body."

"I know. I just want to relieve some of the pull on Huck's injuries."

She uncrossed her arms from over her chest and stretched them out until she could grab on to the sides of Huck's harness and take some of his weight off of the ropes.

"Can you do something for me, Huck?"

"Yes."

"I want you to use your good hand and tug once on that big rope in the middle."

Huck did as she instructed and within seconds they were moving again.

The moment Teri cleared the opening of the ventilation shaft, Millie began crying. Josh drew Teri into his arms and then set her down gently on the ground so he could help Seth Tupper pull Huck the rest of the way to safety.

"Thank you," Tupper said, his own tears flowing freely. "Thank you both."

Millie began splinting Huck's arm and leg the moment he was free of the harness, alternating between working on his possible breaks and hugging the wind out of him.

"You had Mommy so scared. But everything's going to be fine now."

"We'd best get Huck to the hospital in Cairo," Tupper said. "Assuming we can get Mr. Parsket's truck running without the key."

Josh chuckled. "I'm pretty sure I can cross the wires and get it started. While you and Millie get things packed up to go, I'll get the site secured."

"What can I do to help?" Teri asked.

"You," Josh said firmly, "can wait with Huck in the truck."

"But—"

Josh cupped her cheek in his hand, his fingers trembling where they lay against her face. "You are one remarkable lady." Brushing his lips over hers briefly, he said, "I've never known anyone quite like you."

They arrived at the Cairo hospital within the hour. Josh helped Seth carry Huck into the clinic area, she and Millie close behind.

"We're going back to the hotel for a while," Josh said when Huck and Millie had been rushed off to an exam room. "If you'd like I can come back for you, Millie, and the boy in a couple of hours."

"We can get a car home from here, Josh. You two get some rest."

"I'll pick you up at your place tomorrow morning," Josh reminded him. "We'll take care of everything out at the site and should be back by early evening."

"You haven't yet told me how I can repay you," Tupper said. Turning in Teri's direction, he added, "Anything I have, Teri, is yours."

"Like we both said earlier," she assured him, "no payment is necessary. We were glad we were there to help."

Josh opened the door to their hotel room and ushered her in ahead of him. "Home sweet home," he joked.

"I'm usually not that fond of traveling, but I've never been so glad to see a hotel room in my life."

"What do you think, Mrs. Cain, about a nice, hot soak in that huge two-person tub?"

"Followed by at least eight straight hours of sleep in a bed with a mattress instead of a canvas sling," she added.

"Come on," he coaxed, taking her hand and pulling her across the room. "Although, I'm not making any promises about sleep."

She relaxed back in the tub, her back pressed to Josh's broad chest, his arms wrapped around her middle.

"I could stay here forever," she told him.

"Are you sure?"

Josh gathered the soap in his hand and began drawing lazy circles across her chest, soaping each breast with his hand, teasing her nipples with the pad of his thumb. When he slid his hand between her legs, she willingly spread her knees allowing him the access his touch had requested.

"I suppose we could get out," she said, the gentle pressure of Josh's fingers against the very edge of her arousal making her ache. When he surged forward, filling her with the long stroke of his fingers, she sighed and raised her hips from beneath the water. "In a minute, maybe."

He chuckled and pressed his lips to the side of her throat, nipping gently along the side. "Are you relaxed now?" he asked.

Her hips rose and fell beneath the water in time with his plummeting hand, drawing her first orgasm from deep within her body. "No."

She'd barely had time to recoup when Josh slid his hand forward again, doubling his caress, stroking her once, twice until she cried out with a second climax even stronger than the first.

"How about now, my little vixen?"

Rather than respond to his teasing, she rolled over in the big tub until she lay atop Josh's body. Pressing her mouth to his, she took advantage of her soap-slicked skin to skim across his body as smoothly as a figure skater on fresh ice.

His rock-hard arousal pressed firmly against her belly. "How about you, Professor? Just how relaxed are you?"

Josh circled her waist and pulled her farther up his body

until he could take her breast into his mouth and fit himself between her legs, sinking into her as deeply as he could go.

She raised and lowered herself in hurried motions, water from the tub sloshing out over the sides with every frenzied stroke. Once, twice, she climaxed. Josh drew her to him for a deep kiss, and then pressed his mouth to her ear, his hotly worded demand drawing her third climax and his release within the next few strokes.

Josh lay awake long after Teri had fallen asleep. They'd made love once in the tub, twice in the bed, and still he would have gladly taken her again, the only thing stopping him the realization they both needed sleep more than they needed another release, no matter how good it might feel.

He thought back over the long day and of how brave Teri had been during their rescue of young Huck. His heart had been in his throat the entire time she'd been suspended upside down and underground. If anything would have happened to her . . .

Josh shook his head, doing his best to dislodge the picture that had crept into his thoughts. Instead, he turned his attention toward Seth Tupper and his snake of partner Phillip Durning. The items Durning had taken were of relatively moderate value. Josh felt certain if he and Tupper returned to the site tomorrow, the things they could possibly find would more than make up for what Durning had stolen.

He pulled Teri closer to his chest, rested his head against the top of hers, closed his eyes, and willed himself to sleep.

"Good morning," Teri said, running her hand across his chest, threading her fingers through the hairs and tugging on them gently, driving him crazy.

"Did you sleep well?" he asked, reaching out to still her hand and grasp it in his.

"Like the proverbial log. Thanks, of course, to you."

Josh used his free hand to push her tousled blond curls away from her beautiful face. "Glad to be of service."

"What's on our agenda for today?"

"You are going to visit with Millie and Huck while Seth and I go back out to the dig site."

"You don't think Durning will try to go back to grab more pieces, do you?"

"No, I suspect the cowardly weasel is halfway to the far coast by now and arranging passage back to the States."

"How long will you be?"

"We're taking two of the best diggers with us, along with the two who stayed to guard the site. We'll have enough manpower to take down the wall connecting the second chamber room. That's where we'll find the majority of any valuable pieces."

"I thought you hadn't found the entranceway to the second room yet?"

Josh signed deeply, then admitted, "I found the opening the first morning of the new dig. I just kept brushing dust across it to keep it hidden."

"But why? Maybe we could have been out of there sooner? Maybe even before Huck's accident?"

"I needed to size up Durning. I knew he was no good. And, even if we'd uncovered the second room, we'd not have finished excavating before today anyway and it would have only given the bastard more to steal."

"I can't believe he lured Huck into that hole just to distract us so he could make off with the proceeds of the first day's excavation."

"I don't think the fall was intentional," Josh said. "Not that the man's not a snake, but I think he only led Huck up into the dunes to get him lost and distract us long enough to get away. The shaft should have been filled in. The fact that it was overlooked when we switched excavation sites wasn't

Durning's fault. If anything, it was mine or Tupper's. We made the decision to change spots. We should have secured the old site."

"He's still a weasel," she argued. "And if I could get my hands on him, I'd—"

Josh laughed at her obvious outrage stopping her threat mid-sentence. "You know what? If I were Phillip Durning, I wouldn't turn my back on you."

"Damn straight."

He pressed a kiss to her forehead and the slid from the bed and started toward the bathroom. "Get up, my scary little avenger. We've got another busy day ahead of us."

Chapter 21

Teri turned slowly in the cramped foyer of Seth Tupper's three-story home. Unlike Parsket's highly organized and pristine pieces of history, Seth Tupper had filled every nook and cranny with cracked limestone reliefs, chipped urns, and the occasional incomplete canopic jar. The place reminded her of a junkyard for classic cars. The original worth was unquestionable, but the condition of items left a lot to be desired.

"Your father sure has an eclectic collection," she said as she passed through the narrow hallway and into the brightly-lit sitting room.

"That's a nice way of putting it," Millie responded, her laugh letting Teri know she wasn't offended. "He keeps what he refers to as his 'orphans' out here in the open, mainly broken pieces beyond repair and worth very little to a knowledgeable collector. The more valuable items and Dad's precious statue collection are safely tucked away behind locked doors."

Teri took her seat on the couch before asking, "How is Huck?"

"He has a sprained wrist and bruised ankle, but nothing broken thank goodness. The sand was soft enough to cushion the worst of his fall."

"He's a tough little boy. I'm sure he'll heal fast."

"My dad said Josh thinks he's found the opening to the second chamber."

"Yes, I guess he'd uncovered it just before the accident," Teri hedged. "I hope he's right. It would be nice to see your father walk away from this whole ordeal with a lot more than Mr. Durning stole."

"That would make it all worthwhile. However, it'll leave very little for Trevor and his friends to do once they arrive."

"Who knows," Teri said, relaxing back into her seat, "maybe there's still something out there to be found."

"According to a letter that arrived while we were away, he may be bringing an extra student. That will bring their numbers back up to six, including my dad, now that Durning's gone. That's an awful lot of sharing for anything they find once they get here."

Again, Teri thought of the six men who'd discovered the priest's and guard's bodies and wondered if it would be Seth Tupper and his family. As Josh had surmised, they were certainly in the right vicinity and at the approximate time.

Teri pressed her fingertips to the bulge in the pocket of her slacks. The reassuring safety of the *Eye* reinforced her belief that no harm would come to Seth and the others.

Josh unloaded the last of the tools from the back of the truck. Nodding toward one of the nearby workers, he ordered, "Take these canvas slings into the chamber, along with the shovels."

The man backed away, gathering the items in his arms and hurrying toward the opening.

"Are you sure we have everything we need?" Tupper asked.

"If we're missing anything, we can send one of the men back up for it. We should get started, if we're going to get the majority of the more valuable items out before the end of the day."

Josh picked up one of the heavier pry bars and an assortment of trowels and picks before making his way down the ancient stairs. Tupper followed closely behind.

"Where do we start?" Tupper asked, clearly willing to let Josh take the lead.

"We want to clear away the debris I'd brushed over the loose stones," Josh said. "Then, we can get an idea of how many blocks we'll need to remove to get through to the other side."

Tupper stopped just short of where Josh stood and laid his hand on Josh's shoulder. "You had that rascal Durning pegged right off the bat, didn't you?"

"Any man who only judges the ruins by their cash value isn't an archaeologist, or a collector for that matter. He's a scavenger, plain and simple. And, if there's one thing I hate, it's someone who would so blatantly set aside the history of the finds just to line his own pockets."

"If he'd not done what he'd done," Tupper asked, "if he were still here, would you have shown us the other chamber?"

Josh shrugged. "Likely not, Seth, at least not until I'd talked to you privately about getting rid of your partner."

"I appreciate your honesty, Josh."

"What do you say we get to work and find ourselves some treasure?"

"I'm ready whenever you are Josh. And, thank you."

They worked non-stop for the next four hours, carefully breeching the wall leading from the preparation area to the tomb on the other side. When the last of four heavy blocks had been pulled from the wall, Josh was able to squeeze through the opening enough to assess their find.

"We need to remove two more blocks and then brace the upper section with beams," Josh ordered.

"What did you see, Josh?" Tupper asked.

"Enough to know we're going to need a bigger truck."

It was shortly after sundown when Josh pulled the truck up in front of Tupper's house. With Huck tucked in bed for the night, Teri and Millie were on the veranda enjoying a glass of iced tea. Teri stood and went to meet the two men at the gate.

Josh carried a large box in his arms, Tupper a slightly smaller one.

"Keep an eye on the truck, would you sweetheart?" Josh said as he breezed past her.

Sweetheart? The simple endearment, mostly likely meant for Tupper's benefit, launched her pulse rate into high gear.

Josh returned moments later and retrieved another box from the back of the truck.

"It looks like you fellows hit the jackpot," she said as she followed Josh up the walkway. "Is all this from the second chamber?"

"Yes," he confirmed. "There are more items yet to be uncovered, as well as at least two sarcophagi to deal with."

"Did you uncover a Pharaoh's tomb?" she asked, her excitement escalating rapidly with the thought of their success.

"No unfortunately. The chamber belongs to one of Seti I's high priests and his family, and by all accounts, a rather well-to-do family at that."

"Family as in wife, children?" she asked.

"No, most high priests never married. However, they did take lovers. This tomb contained the priest's mother, his brother, and the brother's two sons."

"Not that I mean to sound like Durning, but what's the value of these three boxes?"

Josh shrugged and made his way toward the back of the house where Tupper kept his workroom. "Let's just say, Durning left about a three-hundred-thousand to half-a-million dollars too early. Even at 1920's values."

She couldn't squelch her loud shout of satisfaction, the reaction drawing Josh's laughter.

While Josh and Tupper cleaned and identified the many pieces, Millie began the cataloging process. Teri assembled boxes and filled them with shredded paper.

The first piece they boxed was a medium-sized limestone stele lettered in gold and depicting the priest's family.

The second through fourth pieces were more reliefs, again decorated with gold trimmings and, finally, a collection of canopic jars. Much to Teri's relief, they were empty of any internal organs.

"These are beautiful," she said, running her fingertips across the top of one of the jars.

"Yes," Millie agreed. "Everything is in nearly pristine condition."

"We need to discuss which of these pieces you want for yourself, Josh," Tupper said.

Josh spared a glance in her direction before saying, "Other than one of the mid-value steles as payment to Donald Parsket for the use of his truck and supplies, I'm not interested in taking any of these pieces with me, Seth."

"If not as your share of the excavation at least take something in payment for rescuing my grandson." Turning in Teri's direction, Tupper asked, "Is there something you'd like to have, Teri?"

She shook her head. "However, if it wouldn't be too much trouble, we'd like to see your statue collection."

"My statues? What the devil for?"

Josh met the older man's puzzled gaze and explained. "The main reason we came to Cairo in the first place has to do with a research paper I was working on surrounding an ancient Egyptian curse. I'm trying to ascertain if the supposed statue and stone related to the curse actually exist."

"Well, I'd be happy to show you what I've got. And, if the statue you're looking for is here, you're welcome to it." Tupper turned back to the piece of limestone he'd been cleaning. "Why don't we finish these last pieces, have a bite to eat, and then we'll go downstairs to my storage area?"

"That sounds great," Josh agreed. "I'd almost forgotten

we haven't eaten all day. I guess that's what the excitement of a successful dig does to a man."

Seth Tupper led them down the back staircase and unlocked the first of three doors leading to his storage area. They traversed a narrow hallway and passed through the second secure door. The moment he opened the last door, Josh could understand why Tupper was so protective of his cache.

As perfectly climate controlled as a wine cellar, the room held at least a couple hundred statues made of marble, limestone, molded gold, and ivory. Given there were never any pictures depicting the statue that had once held the *Eye*, Josh had little idea of where to start other than to weed out all but the ivory idols.

"Wow," Josh said, letting the word out on a whistle. "I am impressed."

Teri wound her arm through Josh's and he drew her close. The realization that Seth might actually possess Hatshepsut's statue was even more promising than they'd hoped.

"So, what's this statue supposed to look like?" Tupper asked.

"I'm not sure. The only thing we know for certain," Josh said. "It was made of ivory."

"From what dynasty?" Tupper asked, crossing the room to his worktable, its surface covered in logbooks.

"Eighteenth. According to the legend, it originally belonged to the queen-Pharaoh Hatshepsut but was moved to her stepson, Tuthmosis III's tomb. It was from his tomb that the center stone, known as the *Eye of the Pharaoh*, was stolen."

"If it included a stone, there would have to be some sort of indentation where the stone was placed," Tupper guessed.

Josh confirmed his agreement. "That was my assumption too."

"I've cleaned, catalogued, and stored every one of these statues myself, Josh. I don't recall anything that would fit that description. However, I don't like to second-guess myself so let's take a look at all the ivory statues."

One by one, Josh and Tupper moved each ivory statue from their shelved space to the center table, comparing the storage space number to the information in Tupper's logbooks. And, with each pass, they either rejected the piece or set it aside for further examination.

"This looks more like nineteenth dynasty to me, Seth," Josh said, handing one of the ornate statues back to Tupper. "See the intricate hieroglyphics carved along the side here. It mentions Ramesses II in great detail, and in the prime of his sixty-six year rule."

Tupper made a handful of notes in his logbook and then looked up to meet Josh's gaze. "You are one smart man, Joshua Cain. You must be a leader in your field back in the States."

"Thank you, Seth. I'm not sure about being a leader, but I do enjoy my work."

Josh looked up from his inspection of one of the final three pieces to find Teri staring at an eighteenth dynasty statue they'd already dismissed.

Was she channeling Anukahaten? If so, was Hatshepsut's guardian there to assist with identification?

"Teri?" he said softly, not wanting to disturb a possible connection between Teri and the afterlife.

She blinked once, twice and then lifted the statue into her hands. "Seth," she said as she turned, "it doesn't appear as if you have anything with an indentation meant for a stone. However, if your offer still stands, I'm drawn to this rather plain statue with its outstretched hands."

"I could never make heads or tails of that one. With no inscription, no carving, it was difficult to date. As a matter of fact, if I hadn't found it among some other ruins, I would have likely dismissed it as unimportant." Seth took the statue from her grasp and placed it in a box lined with shredded paper, telling her, "It's yours if you want it."

"Thank you."

Teri took the box from Seth and then turned toward the stairs. "I'm going to go upstairs and see what Millie's doing. Why don't the two of you finish up down here so we can call it a night?"

Josh pressed a kiss to Teri's cheek, assuring her, "We won't be long. I want to review these last few pieces and maybe a few of the limestone before we go."

Josh helped Teri into the truck and placed the boxed statue in her lap before going around to the other side and sliding behind the wheel. The moment the door closed behind him, he asked, "Are you certain about the statue?"

"Yes. Anukahaten came to me there in Tupper's storeroom. She said Hatshepsut wanted to offer the stone to the gods for protection. The moment I saw the figure with its outstretched arms, I could feel a warm sensation wash over me as if Anukahaten or maybe even Hatshepsut was staring down at me."

"As soon as we get back to the hotel, we'll check to see if the stone fits."

She turned to him, her eyes filled with questions. "Assuming it does, what do we do next?"

"We have no choice but to take the statue and the stone to the museum and do our best to convince Dr. Goodson of our beliefs."

"What if he refuses? What if he wants to place the display in Tuthmosis III's tomb instead?"

"Worst case scenario is that he does just that. It will take over fifty years to right it, but at least it will be corrected eventually. Reuniting the statue and stone was what we were brought here to do, and we can ask to go home with a clear conscience."

"Didn't you say in your book that wrongly identified

remains and artifacts were worse than no identification at all?"

"You remember quotes from my book?"

A shrug lifted her slim shoulders. "What can I say, I'm a fan."

Josh chuckled. "A fan. That sounds much better than *groupie*."

She reached across the width of the truck and laid her hand against his thigh. Immediately, his body sprung to life, his senses aimed at overdrive.

"I could be both, Professor, if you play your cards right."

Josh pulled the truck to a stop in front of their hotel, managing to snag a spot just a few feet from the door. "Stay seated until I come around. I don't want you, or the statue, out in view of anyone without me there."

"There you go again, sounding all nefarious, so cloak and dagger."

"Not nefarious, just cautious."

She climbed the stairs to their room directly in front of him and, as he was doing, she stopped every so often to make sure they weren't being followed. The moment they stepped into their room and secured the latch behind them, she breathed an audible sigh of relief.

He made his usual scan of the room, assuring himself that they were alone before opening the window facing the garden to let in the cooler evening air.

"Well," he said when he laid the boxed statue on the table, "let's see if your feeling was right, my dear Neferure." He unwrapped the box and lifted the statue out onto the table. "Would you like to do the honors?"

Teri slid her fingertips into her front pocket and withdrew the stone. "Here goes nothing," she said, laying the stone atop the outstretched arms of the statue.

"It's a perfect fit," Josh confirmed.

The warmth she'd felt in Tupper's storage room came back, washing over her, through her. "Yes," she said her voice a mere whisper. "Anukahaten says we've done a good job."

She and Josh stood toe-to-toe at the foot of their bed. They'd carefully packaged up the statue and the stone together and wrapped them inside layers of clothing and hid them in the closet for the night. Now, it was time to wind down their hectic day and relax, get a good night's sleep.

Yet, relaxing, or even sleeping, was the last thing she wanted to do.

She stroked Josh's cheek, the scruff of his two-day stubble tickling her palm.

"Anukahaten is gone," she confirmed. "I think a little celebration is in order."

"I concur. Where would you like to begin our celebration? Here or in the big tub?"

"I don't think I have the patience to wait for the tub to fill," she admitted. "How about we start here and then move to the tub later."

Josh slid his hand beneath the hem of her blouse, dislodging the front catch of her bra with the quick twist of his fingers, spreading the cups aside with the warm glide of his hand. The moment he enclosed her breast in his palm, her entire body trembled with desire.

In turn, she tugged on the button and zipper at the front of his jeans, sliding the metal closure down slowly, easing it across his arousal.

"Careful," he teased, the single word pressed to the side of her throat.

"Not to worry," she assured him. "I have no intention of damaging the merchandise, especially since I've got plans for it." When she'd set him free of his clothes and taken him into her hand, she stroked him. "Big plans."

Chapter 22

Sunrise came far too early, yet with it a sense of adventure. Teri rolled over in the bed and snuggled into Josh's embrace. This would likely be their last day together, like this, and she had no intention of letting a minute of it pass her by.

"There's no reason to get up early, is there?" she asked when Josh stirred at her side.

"Not before the museum opens, I suppose. Although, we do need to return Parsket's truck and supplies and pay him off with the stele."

"Will we do that before or after we go to the museum?"

"Before, I think. I know it's dangerous to carry the statue with us, but I'd like to have all the loose ends tied up before we make our case with Goodson."

"I'm sure the boxed statue will fit in the tote bag the hotel bought for me after our room was ransacked. It might look less suspicious if I'm the one carrying the package."

"Agreed, although you know I don't like the idea of putting you in danger of any sort."

"I'm pretty sure that ship has sailed. Besides, you'll be there to protect me, as will Anukahaten should we need her."

"In the meantime, I say we get a couple more hours of sleep."

"Sleep?" she questioned, sliding her hand across Josh's chest.

He grasped her fingers in his and stilled her progress at his waist. "If there were any doubt in my mind of you having a previous life, your ravenous sexual appetite has clarified things perfectly."

"It has?" she asked, tugging at her captured hand.

"Sleep, Neferure. We'll make time for quenching your desires later."

They arrived at Donald Parsket's house shortly after ten, the statue and stone tucked away in the bottom of Teri's leather tote. Josh carried the boxed limestone stele in his hands as they approached the door.

"Could you get the knocker please?" he asked, obviously reluctant to let go of his grip on the stele.

She lifted the brass hammer and let it fall against the door. Within moments, Parsket's trusted butler answered the door.

"Dr. and Mrs. Cain," the man said in greeting. "Mrs. Parsket will join you in the library in a few moments."

"Will Mr. Parsket be joining us?" Josh asked.

"I am not certain," the man said. "You will need to ask Mrs. Parsket."

They took the offered seats in the library and Josh laid the box down in the middle of the coffee table.

"Good morning, Dr. Cain, Mrs. Cain," Ariel Parsket said as she came through the library door. "I trust you've brought something for my husband's collection."

"Yes," Josh confirmed. "A twentieth dynasty stele adorned in gold leaf lettering."

"May I see it?" the woman asked.

Josh opened the box and spread the shredded paper aside. "As you can see, the stele is in near perfect condition. The hieroglyphics tell of the birth of two sons, nephews of the high priest who built the tomb from which this was retrieved."

"It is extraordinary. Donald will be pleased."

"Is your husband available?" Josh asked. "We'd like to thank him personally for the use of his truck and supplies."

"Unfortunately, Donald is not feeling well. The doctor has him on bed rest, but I'll be more than happy to give him your regards."

"Yes, please do," Teri said. "We'll likely be leaving within the next day or so and would have liked to have said goodbye."

"Your expertise, Dr. Cain, will be sorely missed," Mrs. Parsket said. "In the short time you've been here, you've made quite a name for yourself."

Josh smiled faintly and Teri suspected he felt a bit embarrassed by the praise.

"We won't take up any more of your time, Mrs. Parsket. If it's not too much trouble we would appreciate it if your driver could give us a lift to the museum."

"Certainly," Ariel Parsket said. "The car will be out front in a moment."

Parsket's butler came to usher them to the door. They'd just reached the entranceway, when Josh stopped to admire a recently added item in Parsket's collection. "This is new," he commented when Ariel Parsket met them at the door to say goodbye.

"Yes, Donald obtained it a day or so ago. It was the last thing he purchased before he took ill."

After bidding Mrs. Parsket farewell they took their seats in the back of the car. Teri clutched the tote bag to her chest, anxious to reassure herself the box was still inside and that they were now approaching the final step in their unusual journey.

The drive to the museum was quick and uneventful. The moment they'd exited the car, Josh cupped Teri's elbow in his hand and gave it a gentle squeeze. "Did you see the limestone relief on the entranceway table?" he asked as they climbed the museum stairs.

"Yes," she confirmed. "The piece looked familiar."

"It should, it came from Tupper's dig site. It was one of the pieces Durning stole."

"Well, at least now we know where he's been, just not where he's going."

"It also makes me wonder if Parsket is really ill, or just avoiding us because we surprised him with our arrival. He had to suspect we'd recognize the relief."

Josh turned the brass handle and pulled on the heavy glass door.

"What are we going say to Dr. Goodson?" she asked, stepping across the threshold and into the museum's marble entryway.

"I'm not sure. I only know we need an excuse to get back into the storeroom so we can get these items into inventory before we hypothesize our theory."

"Dr. Cain." Goodson's grad student met them at the door, stretching out his hand toward Josh. "It's nice to see you again. We'd heard you and Mrs. Cain were out on a dig."

"Yes, we just got back yesterday," Josh said, shaking the young man's hand. "Is Dr. Goodson available?"

"I'm afraid not. He's taken a couple of days off to drive a friend of his to the coast to catch a steamer back to the States. He should be back to work tomorrow."

"This friend wouldn't happen to be Phillip Durning, would it?" Josh asked.

The man shrugged. "Sorry, Dr. Goodson didn't say. Is there something I can help you with, perhaps?"

Teri took a step forward. "Actually, I'm the one in need of assistance. It seems I've misplaced my bracelet and I think I may have left it in the storeroom downstairs."

"Are you sure?" the student asked.

"Not positive, of course, but I do remember removing it in order to keep it from snagging on the crates we were unpacking."

"Your credentials are still valid, if you'd like to take a look. I'm sure Dr. Goodson wouldn't mind."

"Thank you." With his hand at the indentation of her waist, Josh ushered her forward. "We'll be as quick as we can."

"I will need to inspect your bag as you're leaving, Mrs. Cain."

"Yes, of course, I wouldn't expect anything but the tightest security."

They entered the storage room moments later and Josh shut the door soundly behind them. "You're certainly good at thinking on your feet, Mrs. Cain," he teased.

She grinned broadly. "I learned from a master." Turning full-circle in the storeroom, she said, "I got us down here, now what do we do? Without Dr. Goodson here, we've no access to the inventory files. And, we won't be able to leave with the statue."

"I think our best bet is to hide the statue here in storage area and then come back tomorrow when Goodson returns. It's safer here than with us."

"Fine, but where will we put it so that it won't be discovered by accident?"

Josh dragged a chair from the center of the room to the corner. "This building is only a few years old, so there should be open access to the dropped ceiling. If we can remove these panels without doing any visible damage, we can store the box inside and come back for it later."

"I agree. Hiding the statue until Goodson returns does appear to be our best option."

Josh carefully pushed on the edge of the corner panel until he could raise it up a good six inches to create an opening. "This is definitely a more convoluted construction than today's modern tiles, but it's workable. We just need to make sure the surrounding panels can support the weight of the statue." Glancing around the room, he suggested, "Hand me that bookend from the shelf over there."

She lifted the cast iron item into her hand and tested its weight. "It feels quite a bit heavier than the statue."

"Good. If the adjacent panel can manage the weight of the bookend, then the statue should be safe."

He took the square block from her outstretched hand and eased it into the opening he'd created.

She held her breath and prayed the ceiling wouldn't come crashing down. "Does it look okay?"

"Yes. There's no bend." Removing the bookend, he passed it to her. "Set this back where you got it and then hand me the box."

She did as he asked, setting the bookend aside and then withdrawing the brown box containing the statue and the *Eye of the Pharaoh* from her tote bag. "Here," she said, lifting the box up to where Josh waited. "Be careful."

Josh set the box inside the ceiling and then eased the heavy panel back in place. He jumped down from the chair and returned it to the table, releasing a long sigh as he approached. "That's done. Now, let's get out of here and go back to the hotel. We need to decide how best to present our theories to Goodson when he gets back."

As expected, she submitted to an inspection of her tote bag and both went through a cursory inspection of their person to assure the safety of the museum's treasures.

"Shall I tell Dr. Goodson you'd like to meet with him on his return?" the aide asked.

"Yes, please," Josh confirmed. "We have some research to discuss."

They exited the museum and crossed Tahrir Square. She took Josh's hand in hers for the walk back to their hotel. "Are you sure the statue will be safe?"

He gave her hand a gentle squeeze of encouragement. "It'll be much safer at the museum than with us, or back at the hotel on its own. I'm still not certain of how we'll get it added to the proper display, given they've not identified Hatshepsut's tomb as yet, but I'm working on an idea."

She lifted her free hand and laid it against Josh's cheek, offering her support. "You're brilliant. You'll think of something."

The *Eye of the Pharaoh* in its secure hiding place, they completed the short walk to the Cairo Arms hotel. Josh stopped, from time to time, and scanned their surroundings, assuring himself they were not being followed.

Despite his precautions, her nerves were on full-alert. Goosebumps rose on the surface of her skin. And, as she had on prior occasions, she felt as if they were being watched. She shivered and Josh drew her closer to his side.

"Still got the chills?"

"I know there's nobody behind us, but I can't shake this feeling that someone, or something, is watching us."

"Perhaps it's Anukahaten."

"I hope so. I want her to know we're almost done and ready to go home. I'll be glad to get this entire journey over and done with."

They entered the hotel and went straight to their room, checking the hallway twice before slipping inside. As he was in the habit of doing, Josh double-latched the door and then slid a chair beneath the doorknob as an extra precaution. Next, he went to the window and, rather than part the curtains as was habit, he lowered the paper shades.

"Do you feel any safer?"

She joined him in front of the window and stepped into his outstretched arms. "I do now."

Josh lowered his head and pressed his lips to hers, their kiss a silent vow of protection mixed with a promise of passion.

When he deepened the kiss, she gladly accepted the smooth caress of his tongue, the intimate penetration of her very soul. Impatiently, she pulled his shirt from the waistband of his jeans until she could run her hands beneath the hem and across his chest, his muscles quivering with every glide of her hand. When he moaned softly at her touch, she became more aggressive, raking her fingertips through the wiry hair on his chest and teasing his nipples into stiff nubs.

"I need you," Josh mumbled against her throat, lifting her into his arms and carrying her across the room to their bed. "You are my aphrodisiac."

They scrambled out of their clothes, tossing each piece aside with carefree abandon in their haste to be together. The moment they landed atop the bed, Josh pushed forward, filling her with his demanding arousal.

Teri grasped his buttocks in her hands and urged him into an even faster, more frenzied, pace. "Yes, please," she cried out, as eager as he to reach the ultimate pinnacle of their lovemaking. Raising her hips, she wrapped her legs around his waist, pulling him even further into her body.

"I promise," he whispered, his breath coming out in short staccato bursts, "next time we'll take it more slowly."

"Next time," she repeated. "Now, all I want is hard and fast."

Never one to disappoint, Josh gave her exactly what she demanded and more.

Their lovemaking complete, she snuggled into his embrace. Her racing heartrate slowed, returning to near-normal. A soft breeze caressed her bare arms, drawing her shiver.

"Thank you, Neferure. You have made everything right for my queen."

Chapter 23

Teri rolled over in the bed and wiggled her way into Josh's arms, her relaxed state of slumber disturbed by an incessant knocking. Gently, she nudged Josh awake, intending to ask him to put a stop to the unwanted intrusion on their privacy.

"Joshua," Martha called out. "You'd better wake up. Your car service just called. They'll be here to pick you up in thirty minutes."

They both sat up in the bed with a start.

Martha?

"What the hell?" Josh mumbled.

She glanced around the room, Josh's room, at Collingwood. Everything was in order, no broken window, and no wet carpet. It was as if they'd never left.

"Joshua, are you in there?" Martha called again.

"Yes, Martha," he responded, "thank you."

"Oh, and if Miss Hunter is in there with you, let her know her fancy cell phone has been ringing non-stop for the past half hour."

Teri stifled a chuckle and said faintly, "Thank you, Martha."

As she'd just done, Josh surveyed the room with the sweep of his gaze, then got up and went to his laptop.

She searched for her shirt and panties, surprised to see the clothes they'd discarded so haphazardly in the Cairo hotel, folded neatly and placed on the bedside chair. Once she'd pulled the two pieces of clothing into place, she went to stand beside Josh at the computer.

"Any idea what's happening?" she asked, leaning over

his shoulder to get a look at the screen.

"It's exactly as I left it, except the battery is full."

"Okay, we've officially gone back to creepy." Pausing a moment, she asked, "Or, was it all a dream?"

"Were you in Egypt in 1922?"

"Yes," she confirmed.

"Well, it's not likely we'd both have the same dream, even if we were sleeping in the same bed."

He went back to the bedside chair and stepped into his jeans. Slipping his hand into the front pocket, he withdrew a handful of old coins, but no pink stone.

"We've been sent back," she said simply, "but why? We weren't done."

"Maybe it has something to do with not being able to place the *Eye* where it rightfully belongs. Perhaps we were destined to hide it somewhere safe until it could be permanently returned to Hatshepsut."

"I heard Anukahaten's voice last night, thanking us for helping her queen. I assumed I was dreaming, but maybe not. Do you think Anukahaten may take care of moving the pieces?"

"It's doubtful. She may be able to collapse walls, but it's unlikely she'd be able to move the items from where we hid them to the correct chamber."

Teri gathered the rest of her clothes and started for the door. "I've got to get ready for the book signing. You do too."

"And, more importantly, we've got to find a way to tell Mrs. DeChambeau that we no longer have the stone."

She stopped long enough to take Josh's hand in hers, drawing him to her side. She stood on her tiptoes and pressed a chaste kiss to his lips. "Like I said last night, you're brilliant. You'll think of something."

"Did you talk to your daughters?" Teri asked when Josh climbed into the town car beside her.

"Briefly. They kept giggling and muttering something about a surprise and that they only had a half day of school because of the holiday weekend. I told them I'd call them later this evening."

"Even briefly is good, considering how much you worried about them."

"I'm fine now."

"Good, because you and your brilliant mind still have to figure out what we're going to say when we arrive at the museum."

Three hours later, the morning book signing another huge success, they made their way to Mrs. DeChambeau's office. Despite brainstorming on the ride over, Josh was still at a loss as to what to say, how to explain the loss of her husband's treasure.

"Welcome, Dr. Cain, Miss Hunter," Mrs. DeChambeau said when they entered the curator's office. "Please take a seat."

They settled into the two leather chairs opposite Mrs. DeChambeau's desk before Josh coughed softly to clear his throat. Never one to hedge, he got right to the point. "Mrs. DeChambeau, about the stone—"

The older woman raised her hand, effectively cutting him off mid-sentence. "My husband was a good man, Dr. Cain. He was an honest man who only wanted to do right by the history of the ancient world. For that reason, he had his sights set on you and your vast abilities at uncovering ancient Egyptian facts. When the opportunity to host your lecture and book signing was offered to the entire art community, I jumped at the chance because I knew he would have wanted me to."

"Mrs. DeChambeau, while I'm flattered by your husband's regard of my work, I'm afraid you may not be as happy when I tell you that I no longer have the stone."

The woman nodded and smiled, her reaction totally at odds with what they'd expected.

"I trust you and Miss Hunter were able to get the *Eye of the Pharaoh* back where it belongs."

They exchanged puzzled glances, before Josh asked, "You knew?"

"Oh heaven's yes. My husband made two trips in an effort to return the stone, each time leaving him even further from a solution."

Teri shifted in the seat at his side. "Wasn't he afraid of the supposed curse?"

"No, he never once worried about the curse, or his safety, because he knew he was trying to do the right thing. If anything, it was not knowing where and when he'd end up that bothered him."

"So you know about the time travel, too?" Teri asked.

"Yes," she confirmed, "the time travel turned out to be the biggest part of the problem. If he could have only returned the stone to the museum in this day and time, everything would have been fine. However, it seemed the stone, or possibly the curse, controlled everything."

"The stone needed the statue to be complete," Josh explained.

"That was my husband's belief as well. Unfortunately, he was never able to locate the missing statue. He blamed it on his lack of archaeological knowledge. However, I knew he had faith in you. He often spoke of how much he enjoyed your scholarly articles on ancient Egypt. Specifically the eighteenth dynasty."

"Again, I'm truly humbled by his trust, and yours."

Teri grasped Josh's hand in hers and scooted closer to the edge of the curator's desk. In a subdued whisper, she asked, "Why didn't you tell us what was going to happen?"

"I was afraid you'd refuse and then all of my husband's work, his lifelong dream, would be for nothing."

"I'd have never done that," Josh assured her.

Teri shot him a quick smile as if she realized he'd have gladly taken on the challenge, no matter how unusual. Her trust in him filled his heart, his soul.

"So, how did you get the *Eye of the Pharaoh* back to Hatshepsut?" Mrs. DeChambeau asked.

"We haven't as yet," he admitted. "It's still hidden away along with the statue. However, we do have a plan?"

"We do?" Teri asked, the surprise in her voice drawing out his broad grin.

"Well, half a plan, but I'm working on it."

Teri sat opposite Josh on the flight to Chicago, her thoughts on their conversation in the car on the way to the airport.

"We can't continue, as a couple," he'd said. "At least not as openly as we did while we were in Cairo."

"I know. It wouldn't be appropriate."

"Perhaps, once you've gone back to Manhattan and I've returned to Princeton," he'd begun.

In hindsight, she probably should have let him finish the thought, but instead, she'd pressed her fingers to his lips requesting his silence. The idea of spending the next ten days in Josh's company, yet not in his bed, felt like a knife twisting through her chest, stabbing her square in the heart, and stealing any hope of a happily-ever-after from her grasp.

She wasn't exactly sure when she'd fallen in love with Josh, only that she had. She loved his compassion, his wit, his intelligence. The idea of being without him, even for the short period of time until they no longer shared a professional relationship, seemed like an eternity.

When they arrived at the hotel in Chicago, she went to the desk to check them in. She'd barely started the registration process when the excited sound of a young girl's voice filtered through the lobby.

"Daddy!"

Teri turned in time to see two young girls and a tall, very beautiful, brunette headed in their direction.

"I wasn't expecting you two," Josh said, spreading his arms wide to encompass his daughters in a bear hug. Nodding toward the woman, he said, "Thank you for bringing them. I've missed them terribly."

Teri stepped back and watched Josh's homecoming unfold before her eyes. Given what they'd been through, all the uncertainty of what was happening in their absence, she could easily understand his eagerness to see his children.

"Melissa," he said, motioning in Teri's direction. "I'd like to introduce you to Miss Hunter, my publicist. Teri, this is my late wife's sister, Melissa Gray."

Teri stuck out her hand. "It's a pleasure to meet you, Miss Gray."

Melissa shook Teri's hand, quickly turning her attention back to Josh.

"Given it's the holiday weekend, I didn't see any reason not to bring the girls for a visit." Smiling up at Josh, Melissa slipped her hand through the crook of his arm and started toward the elevator. "I hope you don't mind. I requested they move your room across the hall from ours. Unfortunately, they weren't able to move Miss Hunter as well." Glancing back at Teri, she asked, "That's not a problem is it, Miss Hunter."

"No, no problem whatsoever," she said.

To Josh's credit, he broke free of Melissa's grasp. Taking his daughters by the hand, he steered them in Teri's direction for a quick introduction.

"These are my daughters, Mackenzie and Haley. Girls, this is Miss Hunter. She's been helping me with the book tour."

"Will we be able to see your book tour, daddy?" the younger daughter, Haley, asked.

"I'm pretty sure we can arrange it," he said, turning to Teri for confirmation.

"We have two book signings scheduled for tomorrow and a television interview on the Sunday morning talk show."

"Television?" Mackenzie repeated. "Can we go to the studio and watch?"

"I'll do my best to arrange it," Teri promised. Lifting her head to meet Josh's gaze, she waved the piece of paper the desk clerk had given her in the air and told him, "I've got messages to return. It must be important if the boss wants me to call him on the holiday weekend." Patting her pocket to assure herself of the presence of her PDA, she added, "Apparently, it couldn't wait until the plane landed so I'd have cell service."

She handed Josh his room key then, excusing herself, turned toward the elevators, leaving Josh to fend off his daughters' myriad of questions regarding their stay in New Orleans.

That's not a problem is it, Miss Hunter?

Melissa Gray's words echoed through Teri's thoughts as she made her way to her room. Slipping the key card into the computerized entry system, she rolled her suitcase into the foyer and closed the door behind her.

After taking a seat on the foot of the bed, she took out her phone and hit the speed dial. She'd find out what Aaron wanted first and then she planned to do something she'd not been able to do for what seemed like ages. She intended to take a long, hot shower.

Teri arrived at the mall the next morning half an hour before the scheduled signing to assure herself everything was as it should be. Josh and his family would be along at any moment and she wanted to be ready to go when they arrived.

"Good morning," Josh said, coming up behind her. "We missed you at breakfast this morning."

"I grabbed a coffee on my way here." She paused, then asked, "How was your evening with the girls?"

"Tiring. The only time I got any peace and quiet was when we took them down to the pool. Thank heaven for waterslides."

She did her best to force a smile to her face, the picture of Josh, his daughters and the obviously interested Melissa Gray, sapping her usual enthusiasm for a successful signing.

"You're all set up over there." She turned, surveying the area behind where he stood. "I thought your family would be here."

"They're out in the mall, spending my money. They'll be around in a few minutes." He started toward the signing table, but then stopped to ask, "What was so important your boss couldn't wait until after the weekend?"

She hesitated, reluctant to explain the change in the publisher's plans. "We can talk about it later. There's a line forming already. We might as well get started."

"My dad is like a rock star," Mackenzie said, taking a spot at Teri's side. "Everybody wants his autograph."

"Yes," she agreed. "He's the Elvis of Archaeology."

The young girl spared her quick glance and asked, "Elvis?"

Teri hid a laugh behind the clipboard she held and asked, "Would you like to help me with something?"

"Sure."

"Take this sign and put it at the end of your dad's table, near those last few books. That way everyone will know there's only thirty minutes left to buy your dad's book and get it personalized."

The young girl took the sign from Teri's outstretched hand. "When he's done, he said he'd take us to lunch in the food court. Will you come with us?"

"I'd like that," she admitted. "Now head over there so we can get out of here on time."

The mall was crowded with Saturday shoppers. So crowded, in fact, they had to split up between two tables. Josh placed his daughters and their aunt at one table, and himself and Teri at another a few feet away.

"Alone at last," he said when he laid their food trays down on the table.

She met his gaze and smiled. "Somehow, I don't see a crowded mall as being alone."

"Unfortunately, as alone as we're going to get at least until my girls go home."

Despite their previous agreement to take a hands-off approach to their professional relationship, the idea of time alone with Josh appealed to her, making what she had to say all the more difficult. "About that," she began. "The call from my boss last night has caused some changes in our upcoming schedule."

Josh held up a forkful of Cobb salad and asked, "How so?"

"When we reach Boston on Monday afternoon, I'll be leaving the book tour."

"No," he said, shaking his head for emphasis. "I can't do this by myself, despite my earlier claims to the contrary."

"You won't be alone. Our agency is sending someone to take my place."

"I don't want someone else. I want you."

His statement, although meant for the tour, made her heart skip a beat and her emotions soar.

"I'm sorry. I've got my orders."

"What can't possibly wait another week?"

"They want me back in Manhattan to lay out a new tour schedule for another author. Like you, he's written a blockbuster book in his field and, given how profitable your tour has been in just two stops, they've decided to give me a new assignment."

"Who is this new author and what book did he write?"

"His name is Dr. Zackary Pembrook and the title of his book is *Know Your Body, Know Yourself*."

She could tell by the scowl on Josh's face, he was less than pleased.

"And, his supposed field of expertise?"

She smiled sheepishly, certain her next answer would draw an even deeper frown. "He's a sex therapist."

Chapter 24

Teri curled up on sofa in her hotel room, punched the button on the remote control, and poured herself a drink from the mini-bar. The urge to indulge in an overpriced bag of salty chips was foremost in her thoughts.

She'd spent the majority of the evening feeling sorry for herself and wondering what Josh, his daughters, and the clingy Melissa were up to.

A heavy knock sounded at her door, and she pushed herself to her feet, and shut off the television, cutting short the whiny infomercial mid-advertisement.

Checking the security peephole, her heart lifted when she realized it was Josh on the other side of the door. She released the safety bar and pulled on the handle.

"Josh—"

"May I come in?"

She stepped back, and motioned him forward. "Yes, please."

He paced from one side of the room to the other, finally coming to a stop directly in front of her. Enclosing her upper arms in his hands, he traced the sensitive underside with his thumbs. A shiver skittered across her bare skin.

"I want you to call your boss and tell him you're needed here . . . on my tour."

She bit her lower lip and slowly shook her head from side to side. "I can't."

"Of course you can. My publisher is one of your firm's biggest clients. I can have them intercede."

"No, please, don't."

She could see his disappointment rising in the flush of his cheeks, in the set of his broad shoulders. When Josh released the grasp he'd taken on her arms and dropped his hands to his sides, she knew he was angry.

"Why not? Have you gotten tired of me already?"

"No, of course not. There's nothing I'd like more than to stay . . . but, I can't."

I am the author of my own life. Unfortunately, I'm writing in pen and can't erase my mistakes.

How could she admit her past poor judgement? How could she explain her need to repair her professional reputation without telling him all the sordid details of her mistakes?

"Okay, fine." He stepped away from her and yanked the door open with far more force than necessary. "I'll be sorry to see you leave. However, I'm not one to stand in the way of another person's ambition."

The remainder of the weekend went by in a haze, Josh's attention given fully to his daughters. He'd barely said two words to her, other than what was necessary to do the job. He was upset, she understood that, but there was nothing to be done about it. At least not until after the tour ended. Assuming there was anything of a personal nature left to salvage.

The frightening thought shot through her at the speed of light, and not for the first time over the past few days.

What if the wonderful passion they'd shared had only been a byproduct of their unique situation? What if, once the excitement wore off, and the adrenaline stopped pumping, they'd have absolutely nothing in common? Nothing on which to base a real relationship?

Teri shoved the aggravating 'what-ifs' out of her head.

There was no way she could feel so strongly about Josh and him not have similar feelings in return.

There just couldn't be.

When they arrived at the Chicago airport early Monday afternoon everyone went through the security area together, Josh and his daughters first, followed by his sister-in-law, with Teri bringing up the rear.

"It was really nice meeting you," Mackenzie said, coming to stand at Teri's side once they'd cleared security. "My dad says you're a really good publicist."

"He does?" She wondered if Josh's anger had abated at least somewhat.

Haley came to stand at her other side, and stretched out her hand. "Here, I made this for you."

Teri took the braided plastic friendship bracelet from the girl's grasp. "Thank you, very much. I've really enjoyed meeting both of you as well." Turning to Melissa, she added, "As well as you, Miss Gray."

The woman smiled sweetly and motioned Josh to her side. "Josh, if you have time before your flight, I know the girls would love it if you could walk us to our plane."

"You go with your family," Teri said. "I'll get us seats near our gate."

Josh left to escort Melissa and the girls to their plane before coming back to meet her for the flight to Boston.

"Listen," he said, taking a seat beside her in the waiting area. "I'm sorry for being so unreasonable these past two days. I know you have a job to do."

"Thank you."

"I guess I let my own needs overrule my head."

"We have spent a very intense couple of weeks together. Despite the fact that, in the real world, it's only been six days."

Josh chuckled. "Funny how that time continuum thing works isn't it?"

"As scared as I was, I never lost faith in the fact you'd figure out how to get us home safely."

"Like I said at the very beginning, you were just as much a part of our rescue as I was, Neferure."

"I still get shivers when I think about the possibility of being a reincarnated Egyptian princess."

"And, a naughty one at that," he teased.

She felt an overwhelming desire to take Josh's hand. Instead, she clenched her fist tightly at her side and fought the urge. As if he could sense her inner turmoil, Josh took her hand in his and closed his fingers around hers, using his thumb to stroke her wrist.

"You'll do fine without me," she said, closing her eyes and letting the even cadence of Josh's touch relax her. Spoil her.

"Do you know the person taking over for the rest of the tour?" Josh asked.

"His name is David Taylor. He's very good at his job and, as luck would have it, he's a big fan of ancient history, not necessarily Egyptian history, mostly the Roman time period. You two should have a lot to talk about."

"Why do I get a guy named Dave, while Dr. What's-His-Name gets you?"

"Mostly because I recommended him, Dave that is, not Dr. What's-His-Name."

"That doesn't seem fair."

"What's the expression, 'life's not fair'? If it were, we'd both be staying in Boston." She paused and then met his gaze. "I do feel I owe you an explanation . . . as embarrassing as it might be . . . as to why I couldn't refuse my boss' request."

He shook his head. "You don't 'owe' me anything. Whatever it is that's forced you to toe the company line is in the past. I guarantee you anyone who has advanced in their respective professional field has had a stumble or two along the way."

"Even you?"

A deep chuckle filled the space between them. "Hell, I've tripped over these size elevens more times than I care to count." He smiled down at her, and asked, "So, when does Mr. Taylor arrive?"

"He's driving from Manhattan and will meet us at the first signing tomorrow morning. While you're charming the socks off a bunch of old ladies and girls young enough to be your daughters, Dave and I will go over the remainder of the itinerary and my outline for what's worked best so far."

"And, when do you leave?"

"Right after the signing. I'll take the rental car and drive back to New York so I can start organizing the new tour first thing the next day."

Josh turned her hand over in his until he could run his thumb across her palm and the sensitive skin of her wrist. "So, we still have tonight. Together."

Her heart pounded wildly in her chest at the thought. "Yes, tonight, together."

Perhaps, despite their temporary stumble, there was hope for the future. She certainly wished it to be so. Josh was the man she wanted . . . needed . . . in her life. Forever, if it were at all humanly possible.

Josh blew out the candles on their intimate dinner for two and slid the dining cart into the hallway.

"The meal was delicious," Teri said, surprised by the nervous tremble in her voice. It wasn't as if they'd never done this before.

Josh closed the distance between them and drew her to her feet and into his arms. He buried has face beneath the waves of curls hanging to her shoulders and nuzzled her neck, pressing his lips to the rapid pulse at the base of her throat. Gently, he nipped at her skin, the tiny love bite causing her knees to nearly buckle.

"You taste far better than any meal I've ever had," he whispered. Scooping her up into his arms, Josh turned toward the bed. "And I intend to taste every last inch of you."

She couldn't hide the fine tremble of her body, or staunch the goose bumps rising on her skin. The memory of Josh's lovemaking set loose a swarm of butterflies in her middle and made the very center of her being ache with desire.

"I wouldn't mind a bit of dessert myself," she admitted.

"In good time, my vixen, all in good time."

Josh began slowly removing her clothes, stopping with each unveiling to press warm, wet kisses to every inch of exposed skin. When he'd tossed both her blouse and bra aside, he bent forward and pressed his lips to her breast, teased her nipple with the tip of his tongue and then drew her into his mouth for a complete tasting.

She squirmed in his grasp, the sensual pull of Josh's mouth against her breast urging her participation. When she would have drawn him back to her for a kiss, Josh placed his hands at her waist and dropped to his knees on the floor in front of her.

As slowly, as carefully, as he'd undoubtedly unwrapped countless ancient artifacts, Josh peeled the remainder of her clothes from her body, sliding her soft cotton slacks down her legs, followed by the smooth glide of her satin and lace thong. Cradling her foot in his palm, he lifted her legs one at a time and discarded her clothing, leaving her standing naked before him.

He pressed his lips to her lower thigh, just above the knee, and then moved to the opposite leg to repeat the caress with the glide of his tongue against her calf.

"Josh," she whispered. She could tell by the warm flush of her skin her temperature had risen yet another notch. Her heartbeat fluttered inside her chest.

He raised his head and straightened his back until he could press damp kisses to her belly and slide his hands up to cup her breasts. He stroked her skin, used his thumbs to draw her nipples to fine, aching points. When he dipped his tongue into the indentation of her belly button, it was all she could do to remain standing.

As if he could read her thoughts, Josh lowered her to the bed and rolled her onto her stomach, placing her arms extended above her head. With the gentle touch of his fingertips, he teased the backs of her legs with one hand while divesting himself of his clothes with his other.

She couldn't remember ever being so softly seduced, so quickly aroused.

When he'd finished removing his clothes, he stretched out beside her on the bed, the weight of his hand at her waist holding her in place, the press of his stiff arousal against her hip. He began at her shoulders, kissing and stroking, nuzzling beneath the curtain of her hair to place another round of love bites to the side of her throat. Deep within her body, she felt the onset of an internal melting, a climax so emotionally satisfying it almost defied description.

He moved lower on her body, using his tongue to lave every inch of her skin from shoulder to waist. He smoothed his palms across her bottom and pressed a kiss to each hip before moving on to her legs. Every nerve ending in her body sizzled. When he'd finally reached the back of her calves, she was beside herself with hot molten desire.

"Please, Josh, come make love to me, with me," she begged, certain she couldn't take much move of his thoroughly arousing foreplay.

"In a minute, Neferure," he said softly, before closing his teeth on the soft tendon of her ankle and biting her.

That was all it took to incite an explosion within her body, her climax so strong it nearly stopped her heartbeat. "Oh... damn..." she murmured, her softly spoken expletive drawing Josh's muted laughter, along with another nip at her sensitive instep.

Josh rolled her onto her back and then wrapped his hand around one ankle, lifting her leg until her foot rested against his thigh. "You are so impatient, my love. Yet, I love the way your body responds so freely to my touch, the sensual pull of a love bite. I can't wait to watch your expression each time you climax. We've got all night and I intend to spend every hour of it making love to you and seeing that same expression over and over again."

He stroked her inner calf and thigh with the smooth glide of his hand until he'd returned to her ankle. "I've got something for you," he said.

He lifted a rough burlap pouch from the bedside table and emptied the contents into his hand. The cool press of something metallic fell against her fevered skin. It was then she realized Josh had fastened the item around her ankle. She did her best to catch a glimpse of the anklet, yet Josh had begun working his way back up her body, blocking her view. With the first press of his lips to the top of her inner thigh, the gift, as nice a gesture as it was, became quickly forgotten.

"Now, Neferure, let's move on to the next step in that thorough tasting I'd promised earlier."

Teri snuggled deeply into Josh's arms, thoroughly exhausted yet supremely content. Josh had certainly lived up to his promise of making love all night long. They'd made love in the bed, in the shower, on the floor. Josh had gladly demonstrated some of the more complex positions apparently favored in Egyptian orgies.

Her body still thrummed with the remnants of her last climax. Josh had played every one of her nerve endings as completely as a master violinist would play a Stradivarius, over and over again.

"That was . . . intense," Josh said softly, his lips pressed to her temple.

"Yes, extremely intense but in such a delightful way."

He chuckled then clasped her hand and pressed a kiss to her fingertips. "You know, there's not a chance in Hades, I'm going to be able to survive without you."

"But—"

"I'm not talking about the tour, Teri. I'm talking about afterward, when all of this is over. This . . . us . . . wasn't in my plan. I'd convinced myself all I needed was my work and my girls. But you've managed to make a place for yourself in my heart. You're smart, you're beautiful and you're like an organized respite before a mind-blowing storm. I can't picture my life without you."

Romance is tempestuous. Love is calm.

She closed her eyes and let the quote, and Josh's words, sink in to her very soul.

"I agree. I've never felt like this about anyone, and it's not just the absolutely mind-boggling sex, it's everything. Your compassion, your drive, your offbeat sense of humor, I love it all. I love you."

Teri realized the moment she'd said the 'L' word she'd opened a bottle that couldn't be re-corked.

Josh sighed deeply, curled his fingers beneath her chin, and lifted her gaze to his. "There's three words I'd not expected to hear ever again, at least not in regards to a woman."

"I'm sorry, I didn't mean—"

"Don't be sorry, Teri. We'll figure this all out, I promise. However, given we've only got a few hours left before we go our separate ways, this is probably not the time nor place to discuss what the future holds for us."

"Agreed." She laid her hand against Josh's cheek, stroking her fingertip along the thin scar she'd not thought of since the first day they'd met. "Can I ask you how you got this?"

Josh shrugged, the lift of his shoulders evident beneath her pillowed head. "It's not that exciting a story."

"It's not. And here I'd figured you got it fighting off a group of tomb raiders."

"You, my darling Teri, have watched far too many movies." Josh ran his own finger along the edge of the scar, drew Teri even closer into his embrace, and began his story. "I was twenty-two, on my first dig in Egypt with my professor, Ingrid Josephson. We'd barely opened the first chamber in a two-chamber dig when I foolishly thought I could singlehandedly move an oversized mud block out of the way. I lost my balance, fell backward, and scraped my face on an outcropping of limestone."

"Ouch," she said, wincing at the thought of how much both his cheek and pride must have hurt.

"Professor Josephson called me an oaf, told me I had no place in archaeology, and failed me that semester."

"Double ouch! I assume she's since seen the error of her judgment as to your abilities as an archaeologist."

"Not that she'd admit it. I did, however, send her an autographed copy of *The Pharaoh's Mummy* for good measure. A gift I'm sure she'll treasure for at least the five minutes it takes her to unwrap it."

"Speaking of gifts, I never did thank you for the beautiful ankle bracelet. It's so unusual. Where did you find it?"

"In the tomb of Seti I's high priest," he said simply.

She slid her leg from beneath the lightweight sheet and extended her foot into the air until she could take a second look at the gold adornment. "This came from Egypt?"

"Ancient Egypt to be exact. You're wearing a nearly four-thousand-year-old trinket bestowed upon one of Seti's consorts and buried with his most trusted advisor." He smiled rather sheepishly and admitted, "I didn't think Tupper would mind one last reward for all our hard work."

"Oh, my word." She laid her hand against Josh's chest, stroking his fit body from shoulder to hip and back again. Beneath the surface of his skin, his muscles bunched and quivered against her palm. "I suddenly have the urge to say 'thank you' all over again."

"Move your hand another three inches to the south, and I'll gladly say 'you're welcome' in the most inventive of ways."

Epilogue

Newark Airport
Ten Weeks Later

"Dad," Haley called out, "make her stop spreading her stuff all over my seat."

Reaching for the armrest between the two first class seats, he lowered it, effectively partitioning off each girl's private space. "It's a long flight to Cairo. You two need to get along."

"Why Cairo?" Mackenzie asked. "Wasn't this year supposed to be all about the rain forest and limestone formations near Iquitos, Peru?"

He shook his head, amazed as always by his older daughter's memory and grasp of his work. "I'm sorry, sweetheart, but we have something very important to do in Cairo."

Mackenzie shot him a serious frown. "More important than the rain forest?"

"This time, yes, it is more important. We're going to reunite a queen-Pharaoh with a very important piece of her history."

He glanced out his window and then toward the front of the plane before settling more deeply into his seat.

"She's late again, isn't she?" Haley guessed.

"Yes," he confirmed. "She had an important meeting."

"We really like her, you know," Mackenzie told him. "So you'd better not mess things up."

"Excuse me? Exactly how would I mess things up?"

"Let's face it," Mackenzie said, sighing dramatically for full effect. "There aren't too many women who like being dragged all over the place in the hot sun while you search for old junk."

"It's not junk," he reminded her.

"No," Haley added helpfully, "they're arktefats."

"Artifacts," Mackenzie corrected, rolling her eyes in her younger sister's direction.

For the life of him, he would never understand the need for pre-teen melodrama. Checking his watch for the umpteenth time, he silently willed the object of his own life-drama to get her cute little fanny onboard the plane before they were forced to leave her behind.

The past couple of months had been a whirlwind of activity. Teri had designed an extended tour for the sex doctor and then convinced her boss to give David Taylor a second opportunity to prove himself in the field.

The school year had wound down successfully for both himself and his girls, and Melissa had finally taken 'no' for an answer and moved on to her ex's attorney in her quest for a new husband.

He and Teri had worked out a schedule of sorts, alternating weekends between Manhattan and Princeton. In Manhattan, they'd holed up in Teri's condo. In Princeton, the need for discretion sent Teri to the hotel at night while the days were spent with him and the girls.

A humorous thought tickled his subconscious. Just a few short months ago, he'd lamented the thought of a sexual dry spell. He and Teri has certainly put an end to his concern, and in a most delightful fashion.

"Can I get you something?" the steward asked, drawing Josh's attention away from his memories.

"My daughters will have fruit juice. I'd like a coffee, black."

When the young man stepped back to return to the

galley, Josh looked up and met Teri's gaze, her sheepish smile begging his understanding.

"I thought I was going to have to complete our quest by myself," he told her.

"Not a chance." She removed her jacket and stashed both the garment and her briefcase in the overhead compartment then lowered herself into the seat at his side. "If you think you're the only one who's going to free themselves from some old Egyptian curse you're even crazier than you are brilliant."

"I've been called crazy before," he admitted.

She patted his hand in a mock show of sympathy. "Have you put your plan for Hatshepsut's statue in motion?"

"Yes. I've arranged a meeting with the current museum curator. I told him I was working on a paper for *Archaeology Digest* about Egyptian curses and that his museum might play an important part in debunking, or proving, some of the stories I'd uncovered."

"You didn't mention the statue or the stone specifically?" she asked.

"No. I didn't want to run the risk of someone from the museum unearthing the hidden items before we arrive."

"Good thinking. The last thing we'd want is to have gone through all this for nothing."

He settled back in his seat and took a sip of his coffee before asking, "How did your meeting go?"

"Great. You are looking at the new assistant director of public relations for Princeton University."

Josh breathed an audible sigh of relief. "I knew you'd get the job. When do you start?"

"At the beginning of September, just enough time to make this trip, put my condo on the market, and give my two weeks' notice at work."

"Are you excited?"

"About what, the job, the substantial increase in pay, or the thought of being close to you on a daily basis, Professor?"

"All of the above, but mostly the last one."

He leaned close and pressed a kiss to her cheek. Not satisfied with the chaste show of affection, he used his fingertips to turn her head until he could press a kiss to her lips.

"Oh, yuk," Haley lamented, scrunching her nose up for emphasis. "Yuk, yuk, yuk."

"Mind your own business," Josh scolded. As usual, his tone was anything but firm.

"Are you two going to do that a lot?" Mackenzie asked.

He gave his eldest daughter the same frown she'd used on him earlier. "Is there a problem with us kissing?"

"I suppose not," Mackenzie relented, "if you absolutely have to."

He stifled an outright laugh. "Yes, we absolutely have to." He paused, glanced quickly in Teri's direction, and then asked, "Would it make you two more comfortable if Teri and I were married?"

His question drew Teri's surprised gasp and his daughters' mutual smiles.

"Married would be good," Haley said. "Then, Teri wouldn't run away the way Miss Pringle did."

"Miss Pringle?" Teri questioned.

"Miss Pringle was our nanny when the girls were younger. Apparently, she wasn't fond of one-hundred-twenty-degree heat."

"It wasn't the heat, Dad," Mackenzie reminded him, "It was the mummy that fell out of its sarcophagus and landed at her feet."

"Oh, yeah, right."

"The mummy notwithstanding," Teri said, "was Miss Pringle 'fond' of you?"

"As fond as a fifty-year-old woman can be of a man nearly half her age, I suppose."

"Fifty," Teri repeated.

The obvious relief he could see in her eyes, prompted him to ask, "So, Teri Hunter, would you do me the honor of becoming my wife? The name does come with the title Mrs. Doctor." He paused briefly before saying, "Unless, of course, you'd rather keep your maiden name for professional reasons."

She shook her head. "No, I'm fine with being Teri Cain."

"It does have a nice ring to it, doesn't it?"

"Yes, it does," she agreed. "Tell me, Josh, in addition to the possibility of having a set of ancient remains fall at my feet, would this marriage entail lots of heat?"

He wagged his eyebrows and grinned, thoughts of how eager he was to have Teri in his life, spurring him on. "I can promise you lots of heat."

"Count me in then," she agreed. "Even a chance at a mommy would be okay."

Across the width of the aisle, Haley rolled her eyes and gave a short sigh of impatience. "It's pronounced *mummy*."

"Yes," Teri said softly, her gaze locked on his, her smile melting his heart. "Of course it is, my dear."

Also from **Soul Mate Publishing** and **Nancy Fraser**:

HOME IS WHERE THE HUNK IS

When globe-trotting photographer Allison Cain comes home to her family ranch in Montana it's to get to know her nephew and to make amends with the widowed brother-in-law she's left alone to raise his young son.

Evan Carver could never deny his late wife's younger sister anything, despite the fact she's been conspicuously absent over the past three years since her sister's death. Now she's home again on what she's called an extended vacation. Evan's first concern is for his son, Cody, and how his aunt's visit will affect the five-year-old when she decides to return to her high-profile career.

Allison has no intention of going back to work. In addition to getting to know Cody, she needs to confess her biggest secret to Evan. How do you tell the man you've always loved that you're not just his son's aunt, but also his mother?

Available now from Amazon: http://tinyurl.com/hjdvj7y

Author Bio

Nancy Fraser, writer of saucy tales and steamy sex, is the recipient of two 2015 International Digital Awards for excellence in romantic fiction.

Her 2014 novel, *Home is Where the Hunk is*, from Soul Mate Publishing won the contemporary romance category. She also placed first in the erotic romance novella competition.

When not writing, which is almost never, Nancy loves spending time with her five grandchildren and traveling. She lives in Atlantic Canada where she enjoys the relaxed pace and colorful people.

Please stop by her website, http://nancyfraser.ca/ for insight into what makes Nancy tick!

CPSIA information can be obtained
at www.ICGtesting.com
Printed in the USA
BVOW10s0932070917
494197BV00003B/8/P